Dedalus Retro
Dante Alighieri's Publishing Company

Eric Lane, with his wife Marie and four others founded Dedalus in 1983. He has been Dedalus' publisher ever since.

When *Dante Alighieri's Publishing Company* was published in 1985 each new title could have been Dedalus' last book but the company nicknamed by the book trade Dead Loss survived all predictions of its imminent demise and is still going strong.

ERIC LANE

DANTE ALIGHIERI'S PUBLISHING COMPANY

Dedalus

Supported using public funding by
**ARTS COUNCIL
ENGLAND**

Published in the UK by Dedalus Limited,
24-26, St Judith's Lane, Sawtry, Cambs, PE28 5XE
email: info@dedalusbooks.com
www.dedalusbooks.com

ISBN printed book 978 1 915568 17 5
ISBN ebook 978 1 915568 18 2

Dedalus is distributed in the USA & Canada by SCB Distributors,
15608 South New Century Drive, Gardena, CA 90248
email: info@scbdistributors.com www.scbdistributors.com

Dedalus is distributed in Australia by Peribo Pty Ltd.
58, Beaumont Road, Mount Kuring-gai, N.S.W 2080
email: info@peribo.com.au

First Published by Dedalus in 1985
Retro edition in 2023

Dante Alighieri's Publishing Company copyright c Eric Lane 1985/2023

The right of Eric Lane to be identified as the author of this work has been
asserted by him in accordance with the Copyright, Designs and Patents Act,
1988

Printed by Clays Ltd, Elcograf S.p.A.
Typeset by City Printers

A CIP Catalogue record for this book is available from the British Library

To Marie, Anthony and Timothy,
— with all my love.

Line drawings in the text are by Tim Mitchell

DEAD LOSS
LIMITED

Tel 274–0000

The Riots, Brixton, London SW2.

the evening class which started a publishing company

Ref: The Re-Birth of Fiction

PRESS RELEASE
Date 6.1.80

On the 15th January, at 11 a.m., the death and resurrection of the novel will be celebrated on the steps of TIME OUT in front of the television cameras.

There will be a coffin, pall bearers, bookmen and wine. Your attendance is kindly requested at this event, and a good photograph will be had by all.

The question is: What is in the coffin?

FOR FURTHER DETAILS CONTACT DANTE ALIGHIERI ON 274–0000

FOREWORD

There can be few people who are unaware of the tragic death of Dante Alighieri on January 15th 1985. Signor Alighieri was involved in a fatal road accident after a Foyle's lunch at which he was the guest of honour. He was crossing Charing Cross Road to view the window display in Books Etc of *Dante Alighieri's Publishing Company* when he was run over by a Mercedes Benz. His widow, Beatrice Portinari, denies suggestions that her husband was drunk at the time.

"Dante was," she says, "in his usual highspirited rush, and as ever showed an Italian disregard to the traffic."

The success of the Dead Loss imprint started by signor Alighieri is now legendary, with authors like Jane Austen, Anthony Trollope, Mary Shelley and Yoll household names in every land where books are read. But it was not always that way, and the four notebooks signora Portinari gave me to edit show the vast difficulties Dante Alighieri had to overcome.

Where the notebooks break off, Dead Loss, or DL as it is now called, was ready to finish publishing. So this volume recounts the commercial failure of Dante Alighieri and not the success we all know about. Signora Portinari says as far as she knows there are no further notebooks, but she has yet to finish going through her husband's archives.

Originally it was intended to publish the notebooks as autobiography, but during the editing I have reached the opinion that the reader should treat what they read as fiction with a factual basis. The dates are invariably wrong, with Sundays given as weekdays and vice versa, with bookshops mentioned not yet opened, and some of the acts attributed to certain people obviously untrue. So inspite of the objections of signora Portinari and following the advice of DL's legal department, the book is listed in the *The Bookseller* and elsewhere as fiction. Having written the first biography of Dante Alighieri, I thought it fitting to use the same title for this more exciting version of the founding of Dead Loss. If the fictional view proves more enticing and becomes accepted as "the truth", my biography will have to be rewritten, despite being endorsed by Dante Alighieri as the way it was.

Eric Lane,
March 1985

LIST OF CONTENTS

Dedication

To my beatitude, Beatrice Portinari, and the manageress of a certain Covent Garden Bookshop who taught me that there was a fundamental difference between books and baked beans.

THE FIRST NOTEBOOK

Ideas and Decisions

It really was quite boring what was being read. In fact it was rubbish, garbage even. How the person who wrote it could have the temerity to read it out in public was beyond me. But there were a lot of that sort of person around, if the Novel Class at the Art Centre contained a typical cross section of the population. One man was snoring, loudly! At least his snores were rhythmic and kept the listener's attention.

Anton was making his usual copious notes. If I were him, the word crap would suffice. Underlined in red and then boxed round in blue, with impressionistic doodlings in green to add a counterpoint. My God, he's still droning on. Obviously all autobiographical. His wife and daughter were raped by his best friend, Clarence, with whom he slept in his spare time. Kitchen sink and rather sordid. Banal for Chelsea, but a bit yucky for Lambeth and a block of hard-to-let flats.

Imagination and freshness is what this class lacks! My God they're being kind to it! Even the snoring man has a good word to say:

"Interesting to a degree, if somewhat adjectival."

Politeness is not the answer, so I waded in with the truth. The truth falls on empty ears, and the tepid praise continues. A critical travesty, all of this polite banter and I register my protest by going to the bar in the break and staying there. By the time the class had finished I was on my seventh glass of Côte du Rhone.

The Lambeth hard-to-let father wants to engage me in a polemic on his trashy novel but I change the subject to sun flowers and how well they grow in this country. Four glasses of Côte du Rhone later I am still talking — or at least I think I am — without hesitating, deviating or repeating myself about sunflowers. I believe that I must be considered an authority on the subject. I can't remember if I left the bar but as I can hear Beatrice's voice I must have.

2 a.m. I have woken with a most tremendous pain in my chest and stomach. I am in agony and beg Beatrice to ring for the doctor. She has no sympathy and locks herself in the spare room after calling me many nasty names and telling me I got what I deserved. The next five hours are agony to endure as I suffer noisily in almost every room in the house, unsuccessfully trying to kill the pain. The door to the spare room remains closed. When Beatrice went to the bathroom at 7.15 a.m. she stepped over my body without even saying good morning. I crawled, groaning, after her begging noisily for compassion. Beatrice relents and rings the doctor before going to work.

10.30 a.m. I have hyperacidity — it's official! It is an inter-mediate stage on the way to an ulcer. Although I suspect it is a generic term given out by G.P.s to patients with dodgy stomachs when they can't think of any other name. I have I confess very little faith in doctors and believe they have done little to earn the esteem and high salaries the community lavishes upon them. To my mind they are low grade engineers and should have their surgeries in a factory. Some do, they call it a hospital! I laugh at my own joke until my stomach registers its painful protest.

Beatrice comes home at lunchtime and gets my prescrip-tion. I groan gently as she spoons it in.

"I've left everything to you beloved," I splutter between groans.

"Leave your debts elsewhere please," she replied before leaving me for her computer. My imminent demise insuffi-cient grounds for taking the afternoon off. I scream hatred after her, wishing her a long life and a bad stomach.

2 p.m. This is the worst day of my life. My manuscript has been returned. I have not won the DART First Novel Competition. I can't believe it, I really can't. I was so sure that I would. I am so angry that I am oblivious to the pain. It is my soul which suffers now! I will never write another word and in this way take my revenge on DART BOOKS and their readers. In my will I will leave sufficient funds for the posthumous publications of my novel so the world will realise what it has missed. The foreword will explain why I never wrote another novel, leading to scenes of public protest outside the DART Competition judges' homes. Even the double glazed windows will be shattered in the furore.

DECEMBER 1978

I begin attending my law classes at the L.S.E. again. I will it seems have to become a lawyer after all. I copy up the notes for the last three weeks' classes. Beatrice said my parents will be pleased and suggest we drink the bottle of champagne in the fridge that I had bought to celebrate my victory in the DART First Novel Competition. I refuse, full of righteous indignation, saying the champagne will remain there until my novel is published.

Beatrice says fridges only last ten years at the most and not half a century. She laughed, thinking she had said something funny. We are no longer on talking terms and communicate by rude gestures. Women have no understanding, and Beatrice even less than most.

CHRISTMAS DAY 1978

I give my parents indigestion during the Christmas Dinner by telling them the good news. My novel is to be published after all, and soon. My father, says it is not a good idea to publish your own novel. It gives, he said, the impression that no one else wants to publish it. I glare at the turkey before sweetly smiling at my mother as I explain that it is normal to wait years before you get a book published. I have, I said, massaging my stomach, insufficient time to be able to wait. A tear trickled down my mother's cheek, when I said 1980 would, perhaps, be too late. She understands, as always, unlike my father and Beatrice.

"And how will you get the money to publish this novel of yours?"

I feel like losing my temper with my father, and screaming 'from you', but I won't demean myself.

"I will borrow it," I said indignantly, adding, "from a bank."

"From a bank! And what bank will lend you any money to publish a book!"

"Beatrice and I have an account at the National Westminster and I'm sure that I won't find it beyond me to get a loan."

My father begins chanting obscenities in Italian, something he always does when he loses his temper. His Italian grammar is a disgrace to the Alighieri name. Beatrice sends me out of the room to do the washing up. My mother follows to help me and while I curse the tightfistedness of Italian delicatessen grocers she asks how much it would cost.

Perhaps £10,000? Her eyebrows rise and remain high. Perhaps less, £2,000 even. The raised eyebrows descend gently.

"I will try and get the money if you are a good boy and pass your exams." I kiss my mother on both cheeks, dropping the plate I was drying in the process. Beatrice appears in the kitchen and begins yelling — the plate belonged to a dinner set her parents bought us as a wedding present. I'm accused of doing it on purpose, as if I were a teenage vandal sulking as he could not get his book published.

"I'll get published alright," I screamed, "even if I have to pay with my own money."

"With whose money?" Beatrice wanted to know.

"With our money," I replied, my head held high.

"Over my dead body you will!"

"Then so be it," I scream, aiming a left hook, which hits my mother on the chin as she tried to bring peace. Beatrice attacks me, nails flailing, as I try to revive my mother.

BOXING DAY 1978

Christmas was not a success. My parents left without leaving our Christmas presents. Beatrice is not speaking to me because of the black eye I gave her. However hard I explain she can't grasp the concept of self-defence. For Beatrice there is no excuse for hitting your wife however violent she may be.

I'm not looking forward to the visit of Beatrice's parents tomorrow.

DECEMBER 27TH 1978

11 a.m. The black eye looks even worse. I told Beatrice's parents that Beatrice banged her face against the cooker. I don't think they believe me. Beatrice seems happy and is very friendly towards me in front of her parents. In private she tells me that I'm a monster and that she wants a divorce.

I make the supreme sacrifice and say she can have her divorce. Beatrice gets very angry and slaps my face twice. She is too violent for her own good and how I put up with her I will never know. People like Beatrice are a menace to society.

4 p.m. Beatrice's parents are still here! It was agreed that they would go after lunch but all they can do is talk and look at the wedding photos. When Mr. Portinari asked me about my studies, I told him I was thinking of giving up law to concentrate on my writing. Mrs. Portinari changed the subject to pets and asked Beatrice if she wanted a kitten.

9 p.m. They have stayed for supper and even though they live only five miles away act as if they want to stay the night. I look imploringly at Beatrice who turns her black eye towards me.

12 p.m. They have gone, at last! Beatrice cried as they left. The door of the spare room is not locked and we are reconciled as we spend the night in the single bed. Cuddled up together I broach the subject which preoccupies me — my book. Beatrice surprises me by saying if that is what I want it is okay by her. My gratitude overwhelms her and we make love as only Dante Alighieri and Beatrice Portinari can. Our souls float up to heaven, united in ecstasy. Even the bed dances for joy. The world applauds in wonderment as the universe welcomes us up into its stratosphere.

5 a.m. I'm on cloud nine and still rising. Beatrice nibbles at my ear and whispers her love into my ear drum. Our love is too perfect not to bear fruit. We will have a child. *Si cara*, one day we will. One day soon, she replies. *Si amata*, one year soon we will.

I snore loudly and Beatrice takes her pillow and goes upstairs to the double bed.

"I am not, and this is final Beatrice, having a baby, do you hear?" There is no reply, and I wonder if the incredible telepathy we enjoy is coming to an end.

DECEMBER 28TH 1978

Yoll was out, so I scrawled him a message telling him I would make him famous.

JANUARY 1ST 1979

It is agreed Beatrice will let me have her savings and we will try to have a child. We are both indescribably happy and make love "*al fiorentino*". I can now make plans for the birth of a new publishing company which will specialise in original fiction. The idea that Beatrice is infertile is a reassuring one. It took her mother ten years to produce Beatrice so I feel quite safe.

JANUARY 12TH 1979

I saw Yoll at the class and far from being overjoyed at the idea of having his novel published he finds innumerable reasons why it isn't practical. People are so boring sometimes. I tell Anton of my idea. The smile disappeared and he looked as lugubrious as Clement Freud in a television dog food advert. He does however give me the phone number of a chum of his to ring up for advice. At least he takes the idea seriously which is more than anyone else does in the Art Centre bar. They scoff at the name of QUALITY BOOKS and suggest it sounds like a box of chocolates. Other names are suggested with Yoll far in advance with bizarre creativity. SALON DES REFUSÉS and SAMISDAT — I ask you The House of the Rejected and Self Published! We won't get far along the road of publishing success with a name like that. Côte du Rhone fortifies me in my resolve to publish my novel, Yoll's and Mary Shelley's Vampire novel. They'll laugh into their Guinness when QUALITY BOOKS begins publishing bestsellers.

Beatrice consoled me when I went home, saying, "If they don't want their books published, we could just publish yours. It would at least be cheaper." Her loyalty is overpowering. Our eyes exchange celestial understanding.

JANUARY 15TH 1979

I am still attending my lectures although I have little interest left in the law. I had a very interesting talk with one of my fellow students in the bar. He publishes his own law books and actually makes money at it! I tell him that I'm going to do the same but with fiction. He seems dubious but gives me the name of his printer.

JANUARY 19TH 1979

The class is beginning to take the idea more seriously now and I begin to discuss finance. What is needed is about £20,000, which is only £2,000 from 10 people. The mention of money has a sobering effect on those present. Poverty is pleaded by all. I hide my vexation with another futile discussion on what the company should be called. From the pathetic to the bathetic we explore a whole gamut of impossible names.

It was not I told Beatrice a very enjoyable class. I would, I said, end up having to do everything myself. QUALITY BOOKS will end up a one man venture. Beatrice's eyes shone reproachfully. I correct myself, a one man and one woman publishing company.

FEBRUARY 1ST 1979

The first printers' quotations seem to make everything impossible — we would have to sell 12,000 books per title to make some kind of a profit. I feel too dejected to attend my morning lectures but rally in the afternoon and send off for another ten quotations. I prepare a prospectus for potential investors and make up a list of people who could afford to invest in our venture. QUALITY BOOKS will come into being of this I am certain. My mission in life is clear, Dante Alighieri was born to be a publisher. After twenty-two years in academic institutions, from nursery school to a postgraduate law course I feel ready for the battles of the world and commercial success.

FEBRUARY 3RD 1979·

Beatrice is not imagining it after all. She is pregnant. I, at the tender age of twenty-five, am to be a father. Beatrice radiates joy, while I must confess to an overwhelming sense of depression. The Alighieri seed, it seems, can fertilize even the infertile. Beatrice now calls me Dante Superseed. I try to laugh but I can not. I am frightened to tell my parents as I know they will not approve. Publishing companies and children are not what a young barrister needs whose tenancy begins in September. My father just closes his ears when I say the Bar is no longer my chosen career.

24

The birth of a new Alighieri is celebrated with Asti Spumante in the Art Centre bar. In between toasts I map out the publishing schedule for QUALITY BOOKS. Jane Austen wants to know how I will feed my baby and begin a publishing company.

"Nothing," I say, "is impossible for the Alighieri, and my son will grow up to a secure future in publishing."

Beatrice and I stay up until 3 a.m. discussing names for our son. We decide on Francesco. We can not think of any suitable names for a girl Alighieri, so agree Francesco has to be a boy.

Beatrice suggests we should call QUALITY BOOKS either ICARUS or DAEDALUS PRESS. I like both names and ring up Yoll to see what he thinks. Yoll's wife thanks me for my call, but says Yoll has no ideas on any subject at 2.30 in the morning and suggests I ring back at 8 a.m.

The champagne in the fridge is uncorked and the birth of Francesco, ICARUS or DAEDALUS are celebrated. In between little hiccups of joy we make love like Greek Immortals, with divine seed flowing into the infinity of other ages. Our love seems never ending and when I wake at 8 a.m. whispering: "Beatrice, Beatrice, *amore mio*," I find I am alone, my *amore* already on her way to her computer. After breakfast I ring Yoll.

"ICARUS has been used before", he informs me, "but DAEDALUS isn't bad. Better than QUALITY BOOKS at any rate."

I try DAEDALUS out on Anton. He is sceptical and says it's the kind of name Private Eye would soon turn into DEAD LOSS.

I feel frustrated and embittered. Where is the positive attitude, the helpful suggestions and encouragement? I plunge into the bowels of Hell into the gaping jaws of Lucifer, a damned Alighieri! I ring Beatrice at her office, but she is still on her way.

I take consolation in Rice Krispies, at least they still snap, crackle and pop even when they are en route to the devil's belly. Beatrice rings and I cry on her shoulder as far as it is possible with British Telecom as an intermediary. "Why not," said Beatrice, "call it DEAD LOSS then?"

"No jokes before nine please Beatrice."

"But Dante, think of the publicity. An evening class which publishes their own novels and calls themselves DEAD LOSS."

"You are a genius, Beatrice Portinari, a genius."

Oh yes, DEAD LOSS! What a perfect name, success surely must follow with such a name. If Engelbert Humperdinck can make it, DEAD LOSS will. We are on the way.

FEBRUARY 23RD 1979

Destiny is on our side. We have found a printer, William Caxton of Gloucester, and all is now possible. Mr. Caxton rang up to see if we existed, and having heard Beatrice's sweet voice at the other end of the phone is happy to work with us. He wants paying in advance. Credit it seems will come later.

On the same day Mr. Caxton rang, a letter arrived from the L.S.E. about a seminar for graduates who want to start their own business. It seems the Alighieri hotline to the Almighty is still working. The will of destiny was not an expression I used with my tutor, when I told him I wanted to suspend my registration and have the fees for two terms returned. Poverty and fatherhood seemed more appropriate.

He will, he says, press my claim for reimbursement. Being a family man, he knows exactly what I mean. That sounded a bit ominous and I keep wondering what he meant. My tutor was so nice about it I felt positively guilty about not finishing the course, but as I told Beatrice all my mind can concentrate on is publishing. The law of contract means publisher's agreements, labour law not having enough employees to have a trade union shop in the office, whereas the law of international trade, was an impossible dream of dollar royalties on our foreign rights sales. I owed it to myself, the law and the L.S.E. to follow my destiny.

My father will not be pleased — perhaps if I'm very lucky he will not find out. For him I can always remain a lawyer, until my lack of success at the Bar will convince him it is time I tried something else. Beatrice says I should tell him, but I lack the courage.

FEBRUARY 26TH 1979

Everyone is very impressed with my stencilled prospectus, but so far no one has come up with any money. Mary Shelley says she will give a £1,000 which was a big blow, as she has heaps of money. Getting money out of the rich, I have discovered, is very difficult. Yoll, who is almost destitute, has promised £50. But both of them still tend to see DEAD LOSS as something to talk about rather than a serious business venture. Yoll insists still in finding difficulties at every turn. How can we afford an office? Storage facilties? Find book reps? Do the paper work? His objections are endless.

There is no problem which can not be resolved I confidently tell them, but return home full of pessimism. Beatrice's eyes twinkle with consolation and encouragement — just to meet their gaze is enough for Dante Alighieri to have faith and to believe in his destiny.

MARCH 1ST 1979

Beatrice's father embraced me and called me son — I have been forgiven for being a monster who beats his wife. Mrs. Portinari kissed me with greater passion than I have ever seen her kiss her husband. Francesco will be their first grandson. "And your father must be very pleased," said Mrs. Portinari, as she cuddled me passionately in front of Beatrice and Mr. Portinari. I blush with true Alighieri modesty and manage to stop myself blurting out the truth.

"We are all pleased," I replied diplomatically. A little later Mr. Portinari succeeded in getting me out of his wife's arms and into the kitchen. I listened in purple splendour, as he expressed his gratitude and joy in me as a son-in-law, especially at my sacrifice of giving up my LL.M. course to save money for Francesco.

"Not everyone would have done that," he said, tears in his eyes. "And whatever happens Dante, we will stand by you."

There was no mention of publishing in his speech, so I discreetly stayed silent, tears filling my eyes, until we were both weeping.

"Too much Tuscan wine," I said when Beatrice appeared with her mother.

What happened next was something akin to a rugby scrum at school with everyone locked into a communal embrace. I must confess, Italian as I am, such scenes of emotion are a little too much for me, and I pretended to be looking for the rugger ball to hide my embarrassment.

I fell asleep drinking grappa with Mr. Portinari and when I awoke at 1 a.m., the Portinari were still there, so I promptly went back to sleep. As a father-to-be I need all the rest I can get.

MARCH 7TH 1979

I took my novel up to the printers in Gloucester. We discussed print sizes — they seem either too small or too large — and I chose a too large size. My novel is after all a comedy and I want people to see it without a magnifying glass. It would otherwise have been limited to academics who liked to have a laugh — a very small market indeed! After giving the printer a cheque for £1,000 drawn against Beatrice's bank account I was shown round the works and met the staff.

On my way down to London I could not help but think that they seemed too friendly to be good at anything. Doubts filled the Alighieri mind about the wisdom of the whole venture. These continued all through dinner until Beatrice's smiling eyes and two litres of Chianti got the better of them.

There is no turning back now and so I filled in the papers which would turn DEAD LOSS from an idea into a limited company. In a spirit of generosity I asked Beatrice to be DEAD LOSS' first managing director. Beatrice declined, tapping her belly, saying her role was to be the managing director of our family. We both smiled, although I couldn't help but think that Beatrice always chose the easier path. Support was what I needed, not isolation in the board room. Pleading a headache I went to bed aware of what shone in Beatrice's eyes. To have that she must first accept to be the company's managing director.

MARCH 11TH 1979

It seems we need a new roof, if not a new house. We were to quote Toni, "ripped off", by our builders however cheap they were. I now try and avoid Toni, and his nonstop supply of advice, by not going out if I hear his voice. The problem is though he alway seems to be there. No one, I've discovered since I've been around in the daytime, works in our street. Or if they work, they work at home, or like Toni, in the middle of the night. If I'm not careful I will be sidetracked into a society of layabouts and know more about the street's gossip than publishing. Toni seems to know everything about everyone, although he is very vague about his own activities, as if no one can hear him revving up his truck in the middle of the night. I think he has adopted Beatrice and me as we're Italians, and Italians, he says, should stick together.

What makes matters worse is that he insists on talking to me in a language he thinks is Italian. His Sicilian dialect sounds like a flock of larks being garotted. The only reason I manage to understand a word he says, is that 7 out of every 10 words he speaks are in English. He doesn't seem to notice that I always reply in English. I've told Beatrice that I will have to work at her mother's if things continue as they are or start wearing earwax and dark glasses. Knowing Beatrice's mother I'll stick to the dark glasses and the earwax.

I think I will petition the Italian government to give Sicily back to the Bourbons or if they can't be found, the Mafia.

How Garibaldi could have been so stupid to make Sicily part of Italy I'll never know. He is no longer my hero.

Toni asked me today whether Beatrice was expecting. I told him to mind his own business, but somehow the words came out as we don't know yet. When he allowed me to go in I spent a very tedious afternoon filling in forms, begging for money from the Arts Council of Great Britain, The Greater London Arts Council, the Arts and Recreation Committee of the GLC, the Greater London Enterprise Board and Lambeth Arts. Tomorrow I start applying for grants from organizsations on my B list. Happily at the moment there isn't a C list.

MARCH 17TH 1979

My father knows! My mother knows too! I am in double disgrace. I think I will emigrate to South America. My father says, I have brought dishonour to the Alighieri family, while my mother just cries. And all this is just on the telephone. I will never have the courage to see my parents again. Beatrice tells me to grow up and think like an adult and a father-to-be. Between sobs, I explain I am an Alighieri and the son of a good Florentine family and can't bear the pain of ex-communication. I need the love of my parents, their approbation and the £250 a month they give us.

"Sign on the dole," is Beatrice's only reply before she leaves the table in a huff, saying the plates need washing, the laundry ironing and the sheets on our bed changing.

Beatrice is becoming too English. She doesn't understand that an Alighieri does not live by bread alone but by his pride, and the DHSS only provides a giro cheque each month and not the love and affection an Alighieri needs. I would rather starve than live on charity. But as Beatrice's take home pay is over £400 a month we should survive.

It is however a set back for DEAD LOSS, and I must hurry and get all Beatrice's savings before she realises our predicament. I can accept to grow lean from hunger but not to be without my publishing company. For while there is publishing there is hope. A publishable line if there was ever one.

I felt Francesco move in Beatrice's belly and got quite excited. He is a very active little fellow, a real Alighieri. I feel quite proud to be his father. It is a pity he won't know his Alighieri grandparents. He should also be born in Italy, but that is now economically out of the question — Alitalia not providing free flights for Italian nationalists! He will be born in Brixton and be the first Alighieri to be English — the poor boy!

APRIL 1ST 1979

During the break at the L.S.E. Start your own Business seminar I was introduced to an accountant who specialized in publishing companies. I told him of DEAD LOSS and my plan to publish five first novels as a publishing coup. Instead of saying he had to go to the loo he seemed quite impressed and invited me to go to his office and see him. His office is in W. 1. so however good he is, he must be expensive. It is reassuring to be taken seriously by an accountant, especially an expensive one. Hopefully he gives students attending the seminar a discount.

The only thing from the seminar which remained in my mind, was that being a small businessman was a very lonely path, and that if you can't take the pressure you shouldn't begin. Beatrice made no reply when I told her this. All she can think of is Francesco, who she says will be a future managing director of DEAD LOSS. I read the copious notes through that I made at the seminar and realised I learnt nothing, so threw them away.

There is, it seems, no easy way to begin — just get out there and try the ocean for size. The problem is I can only swim 100 metres.

APRIL 10TH 1979

Things are pretty quiet on the publishing front at present so I went in search of work experience and cash. I have found both at the Job Centre, and start work tomorrow as a temporary clerical assistant in the Inland Revenue.

APRIL 11TH 1979

I don't think I'm made for my present position. One hour after starting work I was given a pep talk about working too slowly. By eleven o'clock my supervisor was getting down-right nasty and hinted my career at the Revenue would be a very short one indeed. I tried ignoring her as we, Beatrice, Francesco, DEAD LOSS and I, need the money.

I think my supervisor has it in for me as I'm a lawyer. I belong in court somewhere and not in her office, parading my clerical ineptitude in front of her and enlarging her already oversized inferiority complex. At least this is what I tell myself as I endeavour to work faster.

p.m. (or almost) At two minutes to twelve I'm reprimanded for leaving early for lunch. I return speechless to my desk, tidy it and leave thirty five seconds early for lunch — showing the defiance my family is famed for. My supervisor pursues me out and stops me in the corridor and begins yet another critique of my shortcomings. "Twelve o'clock is not one minute to, but twelve o'clock precisely."

"Thank you," I replied with great Alighieri dignity, "for that piece of information and I promise to do my best to remember it. But it is now twelve o'clock and one minute and twenty three seconds so we are now in my lunch hour." I smiled, as I added. "And in my lunch hour I choose not to be lectured. Good day."

As I left the office her voice followed me out, reminding me not to be late. Any plans I had had to have a frugal lunch were now redundant. I had a very filling curry and chapatti meal, washed down by a bottle of Chablis. Fortified I returned to the office a mere minute late, smiled my way to my desk past where my supervisor should have been sitting if she wasn't out at lunch. My morning's work I put into the waste paper basket to create sufficient room in which to write my letter of resignation. Clutching my letter I went upstairs to what were entitled, Management Offices, and entered a suite of rooms disturbing a dozen or so Revenue men discussing something which my entry brought to a conclusion.

"Sirs," I began, "on behalf of the human race, I, Dante Alighieri, author, publisher and lawyer do hereby resign my post as temporary clerical assistant with Her Majesty's Revenue as from this second. The inhumanity of my supervisor is a disgrace to mankind and I will report Miss Polls and the Revenue to the Court of Human Rights to have you all declared sub-human."

With that I marched downstairs to say goodbye to Miss Polls. Before her mouth opened I closed it with a kiss, and said my last words to her:

"See you in Hell sweetie, in the circle of the Revenue men."

Laughing, I strode out into the pouring rain of freedom, vowing to have my revenge on the Revenue by withholding the payment of my income tax when I received my first pay cheque.

Whatever euphoria I felt waned on the way home, disappearing as I approached the front door, seeing the usual crowd of layabouts righting the wrongs of the world. A mere nod of recognition was the most Toni could get out of me. I decided to cook something special for dinner as I felt I needed to show that I wasn't in the same category as the gentlemen of leisure outside. The smell of spices and the fragrance of the opened bottle of wine failed to divert Beatrice's attention from my news. Her eyes seemed to reproach me as a layabout, a spoilt child who could not control his tantrums.

"But Beatrice you have no idea, it was unbearable."

Beatrice stroked her belly in quiet resignation.

"Dante you don't have to work if you don't want to," she replied, sounding just like my mother when she used to tell me I didn't have to go to school if it made me unhappy, "we can manage on my salary."

"But Beatrice, the future, Francesco . . ."

"Don't worry Dante," Beatrice replied, her eyes smiling like those of a saint, "for the future we have DEAD LOSS."

Only Italian written by a Florentine could describe the sweetness of Beatrice's smile. The English language has the words but not the sentiment.

"*Amore mio, tesoro*," I replied as I tried to kiss every inch of Beatrice Portinari's body.

"Not before dinner Dante, I'm hungry."

As it happened it wasn't going to be after dinner either as my elder brother Giovanni arrived while we were on the dessert course.

GIOVANNI'S VISIT

The sight of Giovanni Alighieri looking exactly what he was, a solicitor, spoilt a perfect meal. I could feel the indigestion rising as another family homily began. As the youngest of three sons, and the only one not to follow the path chosen for them by my father I knew my place and listened in silence to my shortcomings . . . . the pain and anguish I had caused my mother . . . . the betrayal of my father's hard work. . . .

"Are we allowed to visit?" I asked while Giovanni was marshalling his second line of attack.

"I'm afraid not Dante, not yet at least. Papa. . . ."

"Yes, yes Giovanni, I understand," I cut in, anxious to put a stop to whatever catalogue of sins he was about to embark upon.

"Mama would like to see you before the baby is born obviously."

This was monstrous, Giovanni was going much too far; all that resentment he had allowed to fester during my twenty-five years of life was coming out with a vengeance. It seems the youngest and most pampered of the Alighieri boys could do no right. How Giovanni must be enjoying doing his duty.

"Perhaps," Giovanni went on, "a clandestine visit could be arranged if you were very discreet."

A smile of disdain came to Beatrice's lips. She hated the way my family treated me as a baby, and as if in protest she stroked her belly.

"You must remember Dante, it was a shock. Would you like to learn from a certain customer that your son was having a baby. And ... and," his voice dropped almost to a whisper as if he did not want Beatrice to hear, "to be told by the husband of this certain customer, that your son had given up his LL.M. course. The LL.M. course that you were paying for?"

Giovanni went quiet, trying to give the impression that he was overcome with emotion, but really just to savour his triumph.

"I find these things hard to do Giovanni," I replied weakly, "I always have." Both Giovanni and Beatrice seemed to be looking at me with contempt.

"The next time Dante that you have a child, remember you are an Alighieri! We should be the first to know and not the last!"

I nodded in agreement.

"And I, I suppose," thundered Beatrice, "should be the last!"

Giovanni's face showed he would have liked to say, "Yes", but he did not reply, changing the subject instead.

"There is a way Dante to make amends, that is if you wish?"

"Which is?" I asked.

"To take up your tenancy in September and work hard at becoming a successful junior counsel. Pietro and I can put a lot of work your way, by one means or another. You have the chance few have to make your way at the Bar without a great struggle. We have prepared the way for you."

I drew a deep breath while I took comfort and strength from Beatrice's smiling eyes.

"Giovanni the law is a thing of the past for me. It is my ambition to publish books and all my energies are now directed to this aim. I'm afraid that I will never practise law."

"You haven't resigned your tenancy?" my brother asked coldly.

"Not yet."

"Then you still have time to reconsider Dante. You would be making the biggest error of your life. One that we would not be able to remedy for you."

"If it proves to be an error, I will at least be doing what I want in life." Beatrice's eyes shone with joy and admiration, pleased that her man was no longer the little boy of the Alighieri family.

Giovanni consumed his bile in silence, wishing, no doubt, that he could put me across his knee and spank me, as he did when we were children when my parents were out.

"It's madness Dante, this scheme of yours. It won't work — you know that?"

I shrugged my shoulders in reply. "We will make it work," Beatrice replied, "Dante, I and Francesco, we will make it work."

Giovanni shook his head in disbelief. "We won't help you Dante, you know that, don't you?"

I nodded.

"We need no help!" exclaimed Beatrice standing up. "Goodbye Dante," said Giovanni standing up, his fraternal gaze resting coldly on Beatrice. "You'll regret this, Beatrice Portinari."

The firmament shook as Beatrice's divine anger filled the room, before it rose up through the house in its all-consuming passion. Giovanni made no reply, merely shaking his head before he left.

Without Giovanni's presence Beatrice directed her anger towards me. I lacked the energy to join in and sat in silence as I learnt what a baby I was, even Francesco in the womb was more of a man than I.

I poured myself a glass of wine and quietly asked Beatrice to stop. She slapped my face in reply.

"So be it, Beatrice," I replied, and tried to leave the room. Beatrice put herself between me and the door, embracing me with passionate tenderness.

"*Ti amo Dante, ti amo piu che la vita*," she whispered into my ear as her warm kisses covered my neck and face.

"I can't Beatrice, not until I feel more like a man."

Beatrice's hand squeezed me until my manhood cried out with pain and Beatrice laughed.

"You're man enough for me, Dante Alighieri, you big baby."

The ceiling seemed to rotate on an axis of its own as we embraced, celebrating our celestial coupling. We made love "*al diavolo*".

APRIL 19TH 1979

The first time I read through the galley proofs of my novel I got a real kick out of it. The second reading was just hard work. Beatrice read them next and found so many errors that I had missed I felt duty bound to read through them again. To my horror I still was finding errors. Most of the errors Beatrice finds, are also to be found in my typescript, where to my untutored eyes they would have remained invisible, but now leap off the typeset page at me — leap off the page that is, when Beatrice points them out to me.

Full of pain in the head and eyes, the now, we hope, perfect galley proofs are returned to the printer. I felt a sense of pride when I deposited my parcel at the Post Office, as if I was the father of a high achieving child. I still like my novel even after reading it three times within seven days. In fact I find more in it every time I read it, and sometimes laugh so much that I can't believe that I am the same Dante Alighieri who wrote it. I am supposedly the one without a sense of humour in the family.

I find it reassuring that I still like my novel, as it enables me to push aside the idea that I've gone crazy starting a publishing company. The sight of my galley proofs has galvanized Yoll and Mary Shelley into revising their work, and they have even signed contracts. The terms negotiated over Côte du Rhone are quite generous to the author, that is if we succeed in selling any books. Côte du Rhone always makes me feel generous — in future while I negotiate I will limit myself to white wine. It is satisfying to see how seriously everyone takes DEAD LOSS now. Investment is however decidely slow in coming in. I have succeeded in getting Mary to raise her investment to £2,500 — payable in four equal installments — and Yoll, because his great aunt left him a legacy in her will has come up with £250. Jane has managed £100, while Anthony Trollope is down for £1,000, although he prefers to give £500. But as his novel is so long he should at least give £1,000. He is unconvinced by my reasoning. I would be quite worried that all this investment was from the five writers DEAD LOSS was to publish if it wasn't for a great coup at the weekend. An old schoolfriend, who I met up with again during my pupillage, has agreed to invest £2,500. He thinks DEAD LOSS is a dead cert. As far as I know he hasn't a novel he wants publishing.

Yoll and Mary Shelley have chosen the "too small" print size for their books, believing the larger print size would deter the reviewers. A book not being serious if you can read it without difficulty.

We turned down our first unsolicited manuscript on Friday. It really was very poor, despite the author's claim to have published eleven novels. What amazed us more than the unreadability of a published author was how he found out about DEAD LOSS. It seems people with unpublished novels will find a new publisher out, however obscure or unlisted. I tremble at the amount of unsolicited manuscripts we will receive once we get going. Perhaps we should have coupons in our books for would-be DEAD LOSS authors to fill out. An ingenious way of selling books.

MAY 1ST 1979

Beatrice is beginning to look very round. Even Toni noticed and wished us another five like he has. He says it gets easier after the first four. Neither Beatrice nor I smiled. If Francesco turns out like Toni's high decibelled furies, the size of our family will be limited to one. If Francesco is a good boy, there will be more little Alighieri.

I'm getting quite paternal recently and help women with push-chairs up and down flights of stairs and give up my seat on the tube to pregnant women. This is obviously out of fashion as the only person on the tube to give up a seat for Beatrice was a teenaged girl. The gentlemen content themselves with looking the other way.

I am applying for jobs with a vengeance without much success, and am beginning to get desperate. I have even thought of playing the prodigal son and asking my father for a job in his delicatessen. Beatrice however doesn't like the idea, which is a relief as I would no doubt muck it up and only make things worse. I am not made for the role of the prodigal son.

Beatrice has given DEAD LOSS another £5,000.

MAY 5TH 1979

I have sent off Yoll's and Mary Shelley's novels to be typeset, accompanied by Beatrice's £5,000. Jane Austen's novel, a very smart piece of social commentary, with the occasional baby battering scene, follows within a few days. The only problem is with Anthony Trollope's novel, it is almost finished but needs a lot of revising and editing. Anthony doesn't seem in any hurry, despite the lure of fame and fortune. I have offered to edit and revise it for him, but he has, he said, grave reservations about this.

As a covering measure I have looked through my drawer of manuscripts. I have the ingenious idea of publishing my two other novels under different names, so DEAD LOSS could begin with an even bigger bang — six unknown first time novelists. A real publishing coup. The accountant thinks we need at least five novelists to get the full publicity value. I think he's right. He has prepared, as far as it is possible, a projected set of accounts for the first year. The revenue side, he says, is very hypothetical, although the debit side is all very concrete. Accountants I have to admit are all rather depressing. At least my idea to do a back up list of European Classics pleased him.

He asked me what my salary from DEAD LOSS would be, and I shocked him by saying, nothing in the first year.

"Not a good idea, and very unbusinesslike," he replied.

He relaxed a little when I said that Beatrice's take home pay was over £400 a month, and said I was fortunate to have a working wife. I forgot to tell him of Beatrice's imminent retirement.

MAY 12TH 1979

Mary Shelley pulled to pieces the "unsolicited" manuscript I gave her to read, I didn't tell her that I was the author.

"It tries hard, but it just isn't funny. I'm afraid even if this Ariosto is a friend of yours, we can't do it," said Mary emphatically.

I nodded my head in sad agreement.

I read my next best novel out in the class at the Art Centre. "Something from the archives," I prefaced my reading. I knew I had lost the class' attention when the snorer woke up and listened to my reading between heavy yawns. He found my piece adjectival. The Lambeth hard-to-let tenant said he could not believe that such a talented writer could write such drivel. He set the tone and the rest of the class followed.

"Leave it in the archives," Anton said as his concluding comment, "and get on with something new."

I took his message to heart and spent the rest of the class in the bar drinking Côte du Rhone with Anthony Trollope. By the time the rest of the class arrived it was all agreed. I would edit his novel and in return his investment would be reduced to £250. It was a hard bargain, but as I told Beatrice later, I had no choice. It is a good book and we need it. Beatrice wasn't too pleased when I stayed up until 3 a.m. to read Trollope's book. I was, she said, too full of Côte du Rhone to do anything but sleep. My pillow was placed outside the bedroom door.

41

MAY 17TH 1979

Anthony Trollope's 140,000 words of political intrigue set in London and Ireland is now a spry 70,000 word manuscript. I feel quite proud of my recently acquired editing skills and was quite taken back when Trollope called me "an Italian butcher with no place in English Literature". He has refused to contribute his £250, and says if I still want to publish his novel I could claim to be its author. When my eyes lit up at the idea, he had second thoughts, and said I could be on the title page as the editor. One matter he refused to reconsider was his investment, his novel, he said, was investment enough.

Authors I have discovered are a tiresome lot, even worse than lawyers. The page proofs of my "*Comedy*" accompanied Trollope's novel up. November has been selected as the publication date for DEAD LOSS' first list. All the novels have ISBN numbers and CIP classifications, so bibliographically speaking DEAD LOSS already exists.

MAY 20TH 1979

I've found a job for the Summer as a coach courier. My lack of experience didn't seem to worry Rover Tours. They were definitely impressed by my being a lawyer and a novelist, and took the view that Italians were made for the profession, as they called it. I'm brushing up my French, and trying to recall the little German I learnt at school in preparation for my first tour in two weeks time.

Beatrice isn't very keen on the idea, nor to tell the truth am I, especially as Francesco seems in a hurry to be born. Having seen Beatrice's belly grow day by day it will come as a shock to miss the final stages. I told Beatrice I would turn down the job if she wanted. It was then Beatrice announced that she would not be going back to work after Francesco's birth, and whatever I said, nothing could change her mind. I said nothing, aware that yet again I had taken too much for granted. Looking on the bright side DEAD LOSS would at least have a permanent office staff of one. Beatrice has accepted to be the joint managing director of DEAD LOSS. The office, like the warehouse is to be our house. The spare room is now DEAD LOSS' registered office.

DEAD LOSS Ltd., a publishing company, The Riots, Brixton, London, SW2 — it has, I think a certain ring about it.

JUNE 1ST 1979 AMSTERDAM

My tour has been changed, I am now doing a fifty-six day tour of Europe with 54 Americans. Beatrice almost fainted when we parted yesterday, with both Mr. & Mrs. Portinari having to support her.

I am in Amsterdam today, with my pax — travel agent slang for tourists — having a canal cruise. It is a very nice city Amsterdam, much prettier than I expected. When I told Beatrice this on the phone, she got angry, saying I was supposed to be working and not enjoying myself on holiday. I consoled her by assuring her that Brussels would most probably be a big disappointment to me.

I have discovered that I can make people laugh, that is, I can make American tourists laugh, often without trying. Perhaps it is my Italian accent. I just say something like:

"Isn't it pretty, Amsterdam? Aren't you happy that you've come."

And that is it, hysterics of laughter all round. And as they laugh, I laugh, and as I laugh they laugh even more. It is certainly easier work than I imagined being a tour escort.

JUNE 3RD 1979 BRUSSELS

Free time in the Grande Place so I telephoned Beatrice who gave me the wonderful news. My book has arrived and looks great! She was reading it, to see what her husband read like in print. Beatrice said she would mail me a copy to Nice. I can hardly wait.

"What was Brussels like Dante?"

"A bit dull Beatrice, full of palaces and old buildings with everyone getting excited about a statue of a little boy pissing. One of the ladies on the tour made an interesting observation. The boy's a left hander."

"You're not funny Dante Alighieri, you really aren't."

"I love you Beatrice."

"We love you Dante. Francesco sends his love and wants daddy home."

Before I could ask after my infant son in the womb, I ran out of money and had no time left to get anymore. It was almost time for our 2.30 p.m. departure for Paris.

JUNE 9TH 1979 NICE

I didn't sell any excursions in Nice, so the punters — slang for pax — could have a rest and Wolfgang and I could sunbathe on the beach and study the topless situation. Wolfgang is another tour guide and his tour is parallel with mine for the next ten days. He is ever so impressed that I have written a book and have my own publishing company. I have sold him a copy of my *Comedy*, promising to post him one when the book arrives.

Wolfgang has an idea for a book on a place in Bavaria, with an unpronounceable name, that does a Passion Play every ten years. I'm not sure if I'm convinced. But Wolfgang says we'll make a fortune. As Wolfgang is prepared to invest £4,000 in DEAD LOSS I am prepared to take a chance. Wolfgang has a lot of money and says I will if I keep doing tours with Americans. Americans, he assures me, are very generous at the end of the tour.

Beatrice cried on the phone when I told her I missed her terribly and was bored watching half naked girls on the beach. It wasn't, I assured her, all that Wolfgang cracked it up to be. Beatrice thinks Wolfgang is a bad influence on me and the sooner I come home the better. My eyes were full of tears when I returned to the beach, and it was with difficulty that I managed to focus Wolfgang's binoculars on what he termed a most perfect German girl.

JUNE 10TH 1979

My book has arrived and looks great! I signed autographs for the hotel staff before I left and promised to send a photo which they could put up on the wall under the sign:

Dante Alighieri stayed at the Hotel Busby, Nice.

Wolfgang was so impressed that he gave me a cheque for £4,000 there and then in the breakfast room, before showing me where Oberammergau was on the map. En route to the morning coffee stop I circulated my book round my fifty-four punters promising that the copy I would send them would be autographed. A collector's item worth every penny of the $4 I charged. I collected their donations to the Dante Alighieri's fiction fund straightaway before anyone could think up a good reason for not paying. One woman tried to suggest one copy between her and her husband would be sufficient, but eventually paid up for two.

Beatrice always said I could be terribly fierce when I wanted.

Our arrival in Italy and my first fifty-five sales were celebrated with a bottle of Barolo. Although ten thirty was a little early I managed to finish the bottle off. My driver wanted a glass but I refused and he drank his Coca Cola in a sulk. He brightened up when I told him I would give him a copy of my book, his smile disappearing when I told him, I would deduct the price from his bonus.

"Tour guides," he said, "are all the same. Mean!"

JUNE 11TH 1979 FLORENCE

I created quite a stir in Santa Croce Square as I read parts of my book out to the multitudes of tourists, before the police moved me on for disturbing the peace. I was, they said, interfering with the square's other activities of selling leather goods, gold and silver objects.

As a true Florentine I objected that art was more valuable to mankind than commerce: the soul and not the body, the main preoccupation of man.

I paid the 100,000 lire fine with good grace, swearing in the purest Tuscan, never to set foot in Florence again, Dante Alighieri exiled yet again from his beloved city.

JULY 11TH 1979 MADRID

I hate being a tour guide, tourists, travel and the world in general. After forty-three days I and my demented visitors from across the world have given up. Everyone argues, no one cares where we are and some are not even sure what country we are in. Every man Jack of us wants to go home.

JULY 12TH BARCELONA

I had an attack of hyperacidity, my third on the tour. I telephoned London to be replaced, but it appears I'm irreplaceable and must finish the tour. Only another ten days to go.

Beatrice has argued with Toni next door, who has been abusive. It seems we should be grateful that his five little angels climb over the wall and play in our backgarden. If it wasn't for the fact that Toni is built more like a gorilla than a human being I would duff him up on my return.

The news from home is playing merry hell with my hyperacidity. I feel more like a test tube full of acid than Dante Alighieri.

JULY 15TH 1979

My people have finally done it — they rioted yesterday and I had to call in the police. The tour goes on — we are now down to forty-nine people. The extra five seats make the coach a lot more comfortable. Peace has been restored between the smokers and the non-smokers. The civil war has, I think, come to an end.

JULY 25TH 1979

Beatrice and I embraced with such passion that Francesco danced for joy in the womb. The Alighieri family is united once again! I swore never again to leave Beatrice and Francesco. We spent the whole day in bed. Francesco is a very active baby and seems to specialise in back flips.

JULY 26TH 1979

We saw Toni who tried to talk to us as if nothing has happened; that is until Beatrice called him an ignorant pig. He seemed upset as he waddled off towards his house. That afternoon Yoll came round with a bunch of prints from a picture library, and we chose illustrations for the covers of the books.

DEAD LOSS books will look like smart little cousins of Virago, in their snappy burgundy covers.

AUGUST 1ST 1979

I have another tour. A short one this time, only twenty-eight days. Beatrice told me to go to Hell, which is incidentally on the itinerary, being the name of a town in Norway.

"It would be my last tour Beatrice. And we do need the money, and besides think of how many copies of the *Comedy*, I could sell."

Beatrice told me when I got to Hell I should stay there. Beatrice, I think, believes I enjoy my work even though I explained repeatedly that I'm only doing it for the money and for our future. I cannot repeat what Beatrice replied and in English too; Italian swear words, it seems, are too good for me.

AUGUST 3RD 1979

I'm writing my diary as the coach makes its way to Amsterdam. The tour seems like its going to be a difficult one, as no one is laughing at my jokes. It seems that people who take vacations in Scandinavia have no sense of humour. It is also raining.

Beatrice has left me, or at least so she told me over the phone. She is now living with her parents. Our roof is leaking as well. Toni, Beatrice says, has banged holes in the box gutter. But I shouldn't worry about her and Francesco, or the maniac next door with his five little brats, or the leaking roof, concentrating on my Americans, and other important things like DEAD LOSS instead.

I am certain that my hyperacidity is graduating into an ulcer.

AUGUST 5TH 1979

Beatrice has finished work and is reconciled to me again. She will, she says, come and visit me in Helsinki.

I bumped into Wolfgang again, his group is staying in our hotel. He did my Reperbahn excursion for me. It seems there is nothing he doesn't know about it. One girl obviously knew him and called Wolfgang, Mr. 10%. Which was what he charged for doing my excursion. I'm rapidly going off Wolfgang Goethe and if it wasn't for his investment in DEAD LOSS I wouldn't waste my time with him. Wolfgang offered to fix me up with a girl — at a bargain price.

"Beatrice?" I replied, with great Alighieri dignity, "would not approve."

AUGUST 10TH 1979

Beatrice doesn't feel well enough to come to Helsinki. My father rang the hotel five times before I arrived, each time he left the same message.

"DANTE ALIGHIERI, SHAME OF THE ALIGHIERI FAMILY COME HOME AND SEE YOUR SON BORN."

After four months of silence his love has crossed the North Sea to find me. I feel reconciled and overwhelmed by the rising tide of filial and family loyalty. But I can't go home. I must honour my commitments and finish the tour. Even my father must understand that.

AUGUST 11TH 1979

My father is in violent disagreement with his youngest son's sense of honour and says if I don't come home he will come and fetch me. Or at least send Giovanni out to make me see where my duty lies. When Francesco is born, my father will adopt him, so at least he will grow up with a father at home. Beatrice Portinari, my father told me, was too good for the likes of me. My father has obviously been seeing too much of signor Portinari recently. No one it seems understands that a man with a wife and son about to be born and a publishing company can't just up and leave his source of income. It is difficult having a destiny.

THE SECOND NOTEBOOK

The Births

SEPTEMBER 7TH 1979

Tears flood in my eyes. I have held my child for the first time.
Dante Alighieri and Beatrice Portinari have created an angel.
We have been blessed with seven pounds and thirteen ounces
of happiness. Her eyes distil heavenly beatitude just like her
mother's. Thirty-six hours of labour a mere trifle for such a
reward! Beatrice says she will never have another child again,
but she will forget and we will have more.

   Francesco is now to be called Francesca, as the future head
of the DEAD LOSS publishing empire is a girl. She is such
a good girl, not even crying when daddy took her in his arms
for the first time. In fact she didn't cry at all, something that
worries me, as babies always cry in films when they are born.
My father and mother are overjoyed, as are Beatrice's parents
— a child it seems heals all wounds. I've promised my parents
a hockey team of grandchildren — Giovanni and Pietro have
only managed one between them. It seems that it is my
destiny to carry the Alighieri name into posterity.

SEPTEMBER 10TH 1979

It is hard to explain to my English friends what the birth of
a son, or in these liberated times, a daughter, means to a
Florentine.

   Imagine a new star, brighter than all the rest joining the
hemisphere and leading a dance of joy in the constellations.
Even St. Thomas' Hospital in Lambeth seemed to be in tune
with this great event — the birth of Francesca bringing a
smile to the granite facade's dull eyes.

Editor's Note Dante Alighieri continues in this vein for another
eighteen pages, and interesting as it is, most likely, for recent
fathers of Florentine extraction, it does not seem appropriate
to include it here. It is available for the Italian edition of this

work, or as an extract for any woman's magazine which believes its readers would be interested in the raptures of Dante Alighieri, the father of a four-day-old baby girl.

SEPTEMBER 17TH 1979

Beatrice is still in hospital. It seems childbirth is rather painful for women, unless it is a conspiracy by St. Thomas' Hospital to make it seem so. Francesca grows daily more adorable. She has a most beautiful cry — like a sparrow mating. A true Alighieri voice.

The editorial board met for the first time, this eventful occasion taking place in the Art Centre bar. A lot of Côte du Rhone was drunk and after a great deal of discussion little was decided. It was however agreed to write a press release, each of the founding authors to present their version next week. Anthony Trollope, said he was too busy and besides he was a novelist, not an advertising man. This comment induced me to turn from Côte du Rhone to whisky and enlarge my gathering hangover. The high spirits of earlier, when Anton told us that a mate of his, a well known bearded author, would write a piece on us for *The Times*, were by now a thing of the past.

SEPTEMBER 18TH 1979

My hangover politely bade me good morning at nine o'clock. My stomach felt like having a hyperacidity attack but refrained as no one was on hand to nurse me. I drank two pints of milk while reflecting on how hateful authors were in general and in particular Anthony Trollope. I cursed the day I ever edited his rambling sprawl into a tightly contained work of art.

The overwhelming smell of alcohol and nicotine emanating from my clothes made me want to vomit. I could feel the contents of my stomach rising with only the milk holding them down. After emptying my pockets I deposited my clothes on the mountain of laundry I had accumulated in

Beatrice's absence looked like an EEC mountain next to the washing machine.

On a scrap of paper which had fallen out of my pocket I deciphered Anton's handwriting, advising on things to do:

THINGS TO DO
1) Ideas for a stunt or launch.
2) Press release.
3) Use contacts.
4) Write a nice letter to W. H. Smith.
5) Send out review copies to newspapers and radio.

Before Mr. and Mrs. Portinari came round to collect me to visit Beatrice I managed to complete my letter to the Managing Director of W. H. Smith.

Dear Sir,

We are an evening class which has started a commercial publishing house. Our first list will be five novels, all works of original fiction by unknown authors.

Although we are not the usual kind of book to be found in your shops we have noticed that you increasingly stock small publishers and hope you will consider taking our books.

From a commercial point of view we know there is little justification in retailing our books but as the country's leading book retailer with an interest in literature we hope you will take our first list.

Looking forward to hearing from you in the near future.

　　　　Yours Sincerely,
　　　　Dante Alighieri

When I come back from the hospital I will type it up so it gets in the first post tomorrow.

Editor's note No copy of this letter exists in the DEAD LOSS files.

SEPTEMBER 26TH 1979

A day of great joy. At 7.45 a.m. the books arrived, causing great interest to Toni, his eyes popping out as he watched the 10,000 books being transferred from the lorry to the hall of The Riots. I was pleasantly surprised how well 10,000 books fitted into the hall. It is still possible to move in the hall, that is if you move about at a slight angle.

In the afternoon I went with my parents, and Mr. and Mrs. Portinari to the hospital to collect Beatrice, and our little angel, Francesca. There was a problem deciding what car mother and child should travel in, but it was circumvented when I said Beatrice and Francesca should travel in my parent's car and I would go with the Portinari. Having made this magnanimous gesture I still found it very difficult to relinquish my little beatitude to her mother and travel home alone with my in-laws. It was like being exiled from my rightful place in heaven.

I don't know who was the more angry when we got home, my father or Mrs. Portinari, when they had to move sideways through the hall. Beatrice said nothing, but her tears I took to be a reproach. Mr. Portinari seemed to be aiming at me when he popped the champagne, while my father, who even my mother could not calm, wanted to know when I would stop being a permanent disgrace to the Alighieri family.

It was not Beatrice told me later, a happy homecoming. And I should make up my mind whether I loved her and Francesca or DEAD LOSS. Postnatal depression, Beatrice's book says, is very common and husbands should be understanding.

Sleeping in the spare room I dreamt of Francesca and woke up every time she cried. I had intended to sleep outside the locked door of our bedroom to encounter my beloveds when they rose but I kept falling asleep before I could get out of bed.

SEPTEMBER 21ST 1979

a.m. To please Beatrice I moved the books from the hall to the spare room. Beatrice however was not pleased. I moved the books back to the hall. Anyone with a weight problem should just try and move 10,000 books around their house, and his weight problem will be a thing of the past.

p.m. My father arrived, scowled at me, mumbling incoherent swear words in South London Italian, before embracing Beatrice. Calling her the joy of the Alighieri family. He drooled over Francesca's cot, acting like a man besotted. I was ordered to transfer the books into his van outside, they were, he told me, to be stored in his garage. I wanted to object but I knew when it was time to accept defeat gracefully. I transferred the 10,000 books from our hall into the van, under the supervision of Toni next door, who pretended to be tinkering with his truck. I accompanied my father to the garage and unloaded the books. Before leaving I asked my mother to heat the garage to room temperature if it got cold. My father, who overheard, refused to give me a lift home, saying I needed the exercise.

SEPTEMBER 24TH 1979

I delivered the review copies to Media Land en route to the Art Centre and the pre-class editorial meeting. It was thought more would be accomplished without the help of Côte du Rhone. Thirty minutes without red wine failed to bring a decision on what press release to use, so we adjourned to the bar at 5.30 p.m.

The Côte du Rhone brought humour, wit and warmth and an agreement to put the matter out to arbitration. Anton was asked to arbitrate and read the press releases during the coffee break. With Chekovian thoroughness he read them again before deciding that Yoll's was the most appropriate, as it was decidedly different and might get read before being consigned to the wastepaper bin.

Anthony Trollope got into a huff because Yoll's press release was preferred to his. It was, he said, the last time he wasted his time on this stupid venture. Pleading an urgent dental appointment he left as the second half of the class started. I found that I was unable to concentrate during the reading, a sort of *Last Exit to Brooklyn* set in Surbiton. When Anton asked me to comment, I contented myself with a repetition of my opinion of the previous piece on the British in Kenya, saying it was both sober and refined. My comment managed to get the snoring member of the class to wake up, and protest that the piece was adjectival and the images inappropriate.

At the end of the class Anton gave me a list of names of television producers who he said, had been primed, and that I should ring.

OCTOBER 1ST 1979

I have got a little behind with my notebook as life has been extremely busy. I live on the phone. There is almost no one in the media who does not know the name of DEAD LOSS, the evening class which started a publishing company, and Dante Alighieri. It is now almost impossible to get anyone on the phone. The mere mention of my name sends everyone hurrying to the loo or the Middle East.

The media can have a respite from Dante Alighieri as it is time for the big sales push. Despite advertising in *The Bookseller* we have found only one sales rep, and he does Northern Ireland. Jane Austen who teaches English at London University has recruited her students for the London area. Wolfgang Goethe has arrived and says he will rep Scotland, whilst on holiday there. That is a relief as Wolfgang is a pain and a heavy smoker too, and Beatrice is worried if he stays in the house much longer Francesca will develop lung cancer.

a.m. The sales team meets in Knightsbridge — myself and five girls. After a little pep talk we divide into twos. It is agreed that on Day 1 we should do all the calls together. En route to our first call, the Owl Bookshop in North London, we pick up Yoll and Wolfgang who want to take part in the training day.

As sales director I have been elected to do the selling.

Uncertain whether it was with trepidation or elation I entered the Owl Bookshop, ready to open a new development in publishing — the historical DEAD LOSS start. My seven trainées entered behind me surreptiously and mingled with the book buying public, pretending to be browsers and not apprentice reps. This was somewhat difficult as the shop was empty at the time.

With a smile I began:

"My name is Dante Alighieri from DEAD LOSS, the evening class which started a publishing company."

My interlocutor looked sceptical, but I continued producing the five books. "We have five first novels, by five unknown authors as our first list."

The buyer's scepticism widened into a disbelieving grin.

"Normally a recipe for disaster, but mass publicity will turn a dead loss into a publishing success. There will be a feature article in *The Times*. . ."

I continued with great gusto, elaborating our publicity, turning half promises into promises, and promises into reality until not only was my listener impressed but I was as well. With such publicity we will be an unimaginable success.

"We'll try five of each," the buyer said, turning each book in her hand, just to make sure that they were real. "You'll take them back if they don't sell?" My eyebrows rose in astonishment that Kentish Town could possibly lack such enthusiasm in the Arts, that our books couldn't sell.

"They will sell," I replied, chagrined.

"But you will nevertheless take them back if they don't sell?"

"Of course," I replied, "you'll have them in a few weeks. Repeat orders will be dispatched within twenty-four hours."

"Full trade terms?"

"Of course," I replied. I smiled, collecting my books up and made my triumphant exit, followed a bit too eagerly by my seven disciples.

"Brilliant," replied Wolfgang, "really brilliant."

"Have we all this publicity?" asked Yoll.

Oh you of little faith, replied my eyes, while verbally I replied, "I think so."

Elizabeth added, "I think I've got the hang of it. Show them the books and fill up the time with whatever, while they look at them."

I made no reply and we walked, all except Yoll, who roller-skated in advance to Camden Town. The Compendium Bookshop showed greater caution but still ordered — if one of each can be called an order. The buyer was however friendly. He took a shine to *Ireland and Enfields Green* and took five as a parting gesture. In *Writers and Readers* I played the co-operative card, and as a sign of publishing fraternity, they took two of each. Camden Town despite its trendy image seems to be decidedly conservative. This was confirmed when another NW1 bookshop declined to order before the New Year, that is, if we were still in business.

His comment left me speechless and I intended to walk off my resentment, if it wasn't for my trainées refusal to walk to Charing Cross Road.

p.m. We cruised down Charing Cross Road in triumph, Waterstones, Collet International, Books Etc and Collet's London succumbed to the irresistible logic of DEAD LOSS' promotion. The Book Inn showed scepticism but bought, while the Art Council Bookshop justified the tax payer's money by writing out the order before I could open my mouth.

Yoll was now juggling as he rollerskated before the victorious bands of the DEAD LOSS into Covent Garden. We all just about squeezed into the Penguin Bookshop where an attractive young lady with blonde hair and blue eyes told us she didn't see reps without an appointment. I begged, there and then, for one, and was granted one at 3 p.m.

With greater difficulty than we had in entering we managed to squeeze out, Yoll causing quite a stir as he juggled his way up the stairs wearing his roller skates. A tourist, obviously a man of culture, gave him a pound for his performance. We eventually persuaded Yoll to put away his skates and then we entered a Wine Bar for champagne and ice cream. It was, said Elizabeth, just the thing for a celebration. Apart from Yoll, I don't know anyone who can drink as fast as I can, and so when 3 p.m. came I was somewhat merry. I returned to the Penguin Bookshop, with only Wolfgang there to witness my skill, my little band of helpers engrossed elsewhere — Elizabeth and Cecily with two Italians in the Wine Bar, with the rest of the girls helping Yoll perform in the Piazza. They missed the greatest confrontation of bookselling history, which confirmed Dante Alighieri's destiny.

I was not a mere barrister trailing round London without my wig and gown, but a publisher and a book rep par excellence, I had descended down the spiral staircase and looked upon my adversary, survived and ascended upwards to the light of day, purged of inhibitions, and ready for higher things.

Editor's Note: Although not in his notebook, Dante Alighieri refers to his afternoon visit to the Penguin Bookshop in a letter to Anton Chekov, and the relevant extract is reproduced below.

DEAD LOSS v PENGUIN BOOKS

I don't know why I thought women with blonde hair and blue eyes would automatically be ready to embrace the cause of DEAD LOSS without murmur. I was rudely awakened.

"You expect us to buy this," she said, holding up a copy of my, *Comedy* in derision, before handing it around. It seemed the whole Penguin staff was crammed into the tiny office, with only Wolfgang outside to attend to the book buying desires of the foreign visitors to these shores.

"What do you think Hugo?" she asked, as the books travelled round the assembled Penguins to a tall young man with auburn hair, who seemed intent on separating the pages from the cover.

"Very strange little books Liz, not our sort of thing at all."

"Do you honestly expect anyone in his or her right mind will buy a book published by an evening class called DEAD LOSS?"

"We wouldn't have published them and I wouldn't be here now if we didn't believe we had a good product."

"A good product Mr. Alighieri, do you think you are selling baked beans?"

"Books like baked beans are a product which must be packaged to attract the interest of the consumer."

"The consumer? You don't eat books Mr. Alighieri, you read them. What is important is what is inside the covers and not the packaging."

"Then despite our books being funny and little you should stock them, as inside their packaging they are all excellent works of art."

"What do you think Hugo, have we room for Mr. DEAD LOSS on our shelves with his baked bean tins?"

Hugo looked very doubtful.

"If you don't take our books how will you know whether you can sell them?"

I mentioned a whole list of bookshops where our books would be found before returning to the ever-increasing list of our expected publicity. "Not to take our books would put Penguin outside one of the greatest developments of modern publishing."

I don't know if it was orchestrated, but all the Penguins, both great and small, simultaneously burst out laughing. The Alighieri sense of humour triumphing yet again. I joined in the merriment, which extended from the office to the baked bean hunters outside, with Wolfgang leading a chorus of foreign laughter. Further laughter followed as I was asked for our address, and replied, "The Riots, Brixton."

"You really are a joke," squawked one of the Penguins.

"Five of each Mr. DEAD LOSS then, and don't forget to come back after Christmas to pick them up again."

"Thank you Ms. Penguin."

Elated by my success and a swig of whisky from Wolfgang's flask I still couldn't help asking myself why bookshops kept insisting on returning books before they had even arrived. Five books containing Beatrice's cooking recipes or my mother's shopping lists should not be beyond a bookshop the size of Penguin's ability to sell. While great art should disappear off the shelves by the score. We are on the way Anton, I can sense it.

OCTOBER 3RD 1979

After morning coffee in Knightsbridge, the sales force divided into twos, and went off repping. As Wolfgang is a temporary member I accept to be the odd man out and go repping in the distant suburbs of North London on my own. Repping, *tout seul*, can be very depressing! ... the buyer is not available ... on his day off ... after Christmas please ... not our sort of thing I'm afraid ... and you must be joking ... seem to arrive more frequently when one is without support. A not very successful day is brightened by an order and a few cheering words from the *Belsize Bookshop*, we are, he thinks, doing everything right, especially doing our own repping. That way you get immediate feed back.

"Instinctively we seem to be doing the right thing," I told Beatrice when I got home. But my beatitude wasn't listening, Francesca's nappy changing taking precedence.

OCTOBER 4TH — NOVEMBER 1ST 1979

Editor's Note. Although the notebook is full for this period, there is no narrative, merely details of DEAD LOSS' sales performance, so it has been decided to omit these entries.

There is however an article Dante Alighieri wrote during this period which he tried unsuccessfully to get published. It is reproduced unedited below.

DEAD LOSS LUNCHES AT FOYLES

It had not been a good morning. Harrods had turned up its House of Fraser nose at us, while Selfridges had found us not sufficiently interesting to open an account with. So it was not with the greatest confidence that I went in search of an order from the largest bookshop in the world. I went upstairs to the 4th floor to the buyer's office and began my spiel.

"I'm from DEAD LOSS, a new publisher formed by an even ..."

"In the basement please at ten forty-five," the buyer informed me, as he briefly looked up from his work.

"Thank you," I replied, and hastily retreated in search of my fifth cup of coffee of the day.

At ten forty-five exactly I presented myself in the basement of Foyles to find that I was not alone. I dutifully joined a very long line of reps, aware that it was a stationary line. It was not unpleasant listening to the reps' gossip and it made me feel part of a fraternity. I didn't say anything, aware of my junior position in the brotherhood. At eleven fifteen the buyer and his assistant appeared and seated themselves at the table at the head of the line.

It was quite exciting as the line advanced speedily towards the source of orders. Like an actor I could feel my stomach wobble as my turn approached, aware that a very brief period was assigned for my Oscar winning performance.

"We're a new publishing company," I began, "DEAD LOSS by name, started by an evening class. Our first list will receive ..."

"Fifteen of each," replied the buyer, having turned the books round in his hands.

"And where do you suggest we put them?"

"With or next to Penguin," I replied, "that's our market area."

The order was stamped and off I went, elated and full of gratitude to the largest bookshop in the world, and the handsome middle-aged man from Central Europe for his generosity.

It was such a coup to have an order from Foyles that I went next day to deliver the books, my arms growing longer under the weight of seventy-five paper back books.

Having wandered aimlessly around the bookshop I finally found the store room.

"Where do you want them?" I asked.

"Anywhere you like," replied an Australian voice, his mouth full of vol-au vent. "Are you hungry?" he asked, pointing to the tray of hors d'oeuvres.

"Help yourself, they're on the house. It's either you or the dustbin."

"Thanks," I replied, digging into the canapes. As I munched on the generosity of Foyles, a young girl appeared with four more trays, from on high.

"Would you like a party?" I asked, "because I could nip out and buy a bottle."

"Good on yer mate," replied the packer. The young girl also smiled approvingly, obviously the wine beginning and ending upstairs.

I returned with a two litre flask of my native vintage, Chianti. The news of the party must have spread as the packers had tripled and the office staff quadrupled. A pleasant hour was spent amongst the foothills of Tuscany, as the canapes were consumed with gusto.

My Australian friend Bruce, advised me to put my books out, saying that was what all the reps did.

"Good on you Bruce," I replied gratefully, disappearing nimbly with my elongated arms into the fiction department. I spent a pleasant twenty minutes rearranging the Penguin display to incorporate our books. The distinctive tone of the DEAD LOSS burgundy was nicely set off by the whites and muted colours of Penguin. All our books were face out, and each title was put in five different places, so as to heighten the effect. For my own book, I went even further, putting a few copies next to Jackie Collins in the Pan section, feeling I belonged more with the bestsellers than the literati.

Looking carefully around, I took advantage of the assistant's temporary absence to place a copy of each of our books in the window. Again the vivid burgundy enlivened the display, and I spent a good ten minutes entranced in front of Foyles, admiring my product. Perhaps if baked beans were in burgundy tins they would sell more. When I informed the cohorts of the DEAD LOSS of our Foyles display they made their way up to Charing Cross Road to admire my handiwork.

A few weeks later I returned to see how well we were selling and failed to find a single copy on the shelves. I asked everyone but no one could even remember us, let alone tell me where our books were. I searched every inch of the fiction and literature departments before I concluded our books were not to be found. I had to admit that I expected foul play from the Penguin rep and it was with hate in my heart that I descended to the basement.

When my turn came I presented our five books again.

"Our latest books," I said.

The books were looked at in the usual manner.

"Ten of each."

"But last time you took fifteen."

The buyer looked up and smiled sardonically. "But this time we'll take ten."

I remembered my place and smiled gratefully.

"How many titles have you now?"

"Ten," I replied.

"Then you must buy a shelf."

I felt my knees turn to jelly as I turned pale. I wanted to be honest and tell the truth — we weren't ready for such an honour. All our honours had to be free with no strings attached.

"Can't we go back with Penguin like last time."

"No, this time you must buy your shelf."

"Thank you," I replied, my palms clammy with perspiration.

"A small shelf," he added, "and if things go well you can get a bigger one later."

"Yes, we would be happy with a small one. Anything would do."

"Wait till the end and we'll arrange things."

I nodded gratefully, watching shyly, as order after order got stamped. I worked out the way I would turn down Foyle's magnanimous offer ... "We're such a small publisher that I really don't think ..." but the words came out as, "Thank you", as I followed the buyer upstairs. A shelf, a rather good one, well sited near our former position in Penguin was provided and I was left with the young man who rang the fiction department. I showed him our books, and he seemed most impressed; impressed enough to alter the ten to twenty. My eyes lit up with pleasure and I almost ran to the underground in my haste to get home to The Riots, so eager was I to fill our shelf.

It was a joke after all, you didn't have to buy space in Foyles.

While I was artistically arranging our titles on the DEAD LOSS shelf a sudden fear assailed me — what if the books didn't sell? They would stare out forever from our shelf until they decomposed. There would be no kindly Penguin rep to make them disappear. It was madness, the whole DEAD LOSS business and I wished for my wig and gown and the safety of the Inns of Court. My eyes caught sight of my *Comedy* smiling down at me from the shelf and I thought of Beatrice and Francesca at home. All doubts disappeared. Here was my destiny.

I had had my first Foyles lunch, and there would be a second, but this time not in the basement, with Foyles supplying the wine. I would be back as an honoured guest, the managing director of a major publishing company, who as it behoved a gentleman of culture, wrote novels of quality in his spare time. Cristina and I would eat lunch together amongst the literati, the fate of Foyles and DEAD LOSS inextricably mixed.

NOVEMBER 2ND 1979

a.m. Beatrice gave me a nappy changing lesson — my sixth — but I still can't get the hang of it. Francesca cries and wriggles and my hands get clumsy and the nappy comes undone. Beatrice thinks I lack manual dexterity, at least she says that when she's in a good mood. When she is angry, she tells me, I must be the most stupid man in the world as I can't change a little baby's nappy. And when there is a board meeting she'll tell our fellow directors of my ineptitude and I'll see how their confidence in me will disappear.

"Would you," Beatrice said, "trust a man with your investments who could not change a nappy after six lessons?"

I tried to change the subject by remarking that Francesca's pooh was very gooey. It wasn't as it proved the right thing to have said. It seems it is only gooey as Francesca is breast fed and I am a fascist who wants to deprive his child of her mother's milk.

It is hard to be a father and a good husband when your wife despises you. I read Beatrice's book again, eager to learn when postnatal depression ends and a husband can stop being understanding.

I'm booked in for my seventh lesson but am allowed out to see W. H. Smith on the understanding I will try and do better in my nappy changing.

p.m. As I sat in the senior buyer's office I felt quite inhibited. This was not like going into a bookshop however large, but a trip into the world of big business. Thousands of people worked in this building, it had a foyer with security attendants, the man I was talking to had assistants, secretaries, office seniors and juniors at his disposition, while I had the spare room of The Riots and a staff, when it was there, of one adult and one child. I was happy that the managing director was too busy to see me, the senior buyer was honour enough. I felt mesmerized by the smiling face in front of me as I learnt about the complexities of book retailing.

He was so nice and the atmosphere so pleasant I relaxed, enjoying an interesting conversation. If it would not have seemed gauche I would have pulled out my notebook and made notes. While I was wishing our conversation would last all afternoon, a question emerged from out of our discourse.

"What is there about your books that is different?"

I felt unprepared for any questions, especially difficult ones and felt I was growing red as I dithered in painful silence. The senior buyer had heard my spiel, he knew it all, but still wanted more. My mouth opened and words came out, wave upon wave of platitudes. Defeat listened politely, ready to show the failed publisher the door.

"Reader criteria," I said, "we use reader criteria. We are not in the business of publishing fashions or predicting what will sell tomorrow, but of publishing books which we, as readers, have enjoyed. If novels on rabbits are out of fashion and we are offered a superb book on rabbits we will publish it. There is always room for one more, if it is good enough."

We exchanged smiles, my eyes ablaze with inspiration. I had, I felt, passed whatever exam it was that I had been set. Another buyer was called in, a young woman, again wearing a big smile, as if they were obligatory in Strand House, and we were introduced.

"The good news," said the senior buyer, "is that we will take your books." My heart soared into the stratosphere. We had made it. The big time beckoned.

"The bad news is the terms. We expect 50% discount, and will return after three months or so all unsold books whatever condition they are in."

My heart returned rather dismayed from its trip to the stratosphere. I now knew why everyone connected to W. H. Smith could afford a big smile.

"We will take 500 copies of each title, and the books must arrive at our warehouse in Swindon fifteen days before publication."

My heart returned to the stratosphere as I computed that I had just sold two thousand five hundred books.

On my return home I wrote an identical letter to Menzies and Boots as I did to W. H. Smith, rather liking the idea of further mass sales. Beatrice congratulated me by greater patience during my seventh nappy changing lesson.

"Just imagine Dante that W. H. Smith is Francesca and wants his nappy changed, and if you do it well, he will order a million books."

Yoll and Elizabeth were distributing the books in London, while I went out to see the owner of a chain of bookshops.

"You are very brave to be a publisher," he said, "and as I admire bravery I will stock your books in my shops."

I smiled feeling far from brave.

"What terms do you offer?"

"Thirty-five per cent."

He shook his head vehemently.

"Bearing in mind the number of your shops, we could go up to forty per cent?"

"Forty-five per cent is what we normally expect from publishers."

"We couldn't give that. Not that is, if you don't order 500 copies of each title."

"We couldn't manage anything like that. What do you say we split the difference?"

I nodded in agreement.

"Forty-three per cent, and a favourable policy on returns?"

I nodded, far from happy. Soon it would be easier to have DEAD LOSS registered as a charity, giving a full one hundred per cent discount to bookshops.

I cheered up during the afternoon when I got an order from Hatchards, happy in the knowledge that the Queen could now buy our books, cutting down the number of complimentary copies by one.

NOVEMBER 5TH 1979

We had our first full board meeting and it was decided to have a launch event. We would take the publishing world by storm on November 17th, Beatrice's birthday. I was appointed organization's director, making me the sales director, publicity director, distribution director, as well as one of the managing directors. I wonder sometimes whether anyone else wants to do anything for DEAD LOSS. I seem to be the only working director.

NOVEMBER 6TH 1979

Wolfgang Goethe went on holiday to Scotland. We prepared a special scenic route for him, so that he could deliver the books to W. H. Smith in Swindon, and rep Bristol, Cardiff and Chester on the way. In Scotland he is to rep Glasgow and Edinburgh, in between sightseeing trips.

Once Wolfgang left I felt quite attached to him, and despite three cans of air freshener his smell still lingers on in the spare room. Wolfgang rang up from Bristol and gave details of his three orders, inducing brotherly love for his devotion to the cause.

NOVEMBER 8TH 1979

I confided to Anton Chekov before the class that I just couldn't think of anything for a launch event. Anton suggested something to do with death and rebirth: the novel coming alive through DEAD LOSS.

During the break I rang Beatrice who liked the idea of a girl jumping out of a coffin in Covent Garden. It was, she said, a great idea.

NOVEMBER 9TH 1979

Elizabeth isn't happy that she has been selected to be the girl to jump out of the coffin. To make it more attractive I offered her £10. She is thinking about it. Yoll, DEAD LOSS' official press release man dropped in the launch press release, which, after having it duplicated, I delivered to the media by hand.

John Menzies replied thanking me for my letter, but declined to take our books. Boots had already turned us down the day before. My loyalty as a book buyer is now and forever more with W. H. Smith, I told Beatrice, while she was breastfeeding Francesca. We will make, my beatitude, W. H. Smith rich and proud that they were in at the start of the DEAD LOSS epic.

NOVEMBER 10TH 1979

Mary Shelley, true to her promise, had the coffin delivered to The Riots. Toni who was driving the other way down the road, stopped his truck and reversed just in time to see the coffin enter our house. He stayed outside all morning waiting to see if it came out, and when he disappeared he had one of his little brats keep watch. Toni's children attend school like Toni works, which explains why their English resembles Toni's Sicilian.

The coffin looked real, which in a way it was, although it was only a theatrical prop in a play in which Mary Shelley had a small part. During the afternoon we practised carrying Elizabeth round The Riots in the coffin and ran through the stunt. At five the coffin was collected for the evening performance. It's departure watched by Toni and his family with their mouths opened wide.

NOVEMBER 11TH 1979

A nice piece appeared about DEAD LOSS in *The Bookseller*. It was our first piece of publicity. I live on the phone again. As soon as I put the phone down the phone rings again. The interest from Media Land is phenomenal. I feel like a publishing superstar. I did my *Times* interview today, and feel very important.

NOVEMBER 12TH 1979

The BBC and ITV rang. I almost fainted. People working in television actually ringing me up at The Riots. We could be on five television programmes, and on Radio 4, 2 and 1. It is just like a dream, the sort you want to go on forever but eventually wake up from. We will be rich and famous!

The publicity wheeze of the century. Elated I ring up the printer and order an immediate reprint, another five thousand of each title. We are on the way!

NOVEMBER 13TH 1979

Beatrice and I argue over Francesca crying while I'm on the phone to the BBC. Beatrice says Francesca has as much right as I have to use the spare room, and the BBC have babies too. Sometimes I think Beatrice is trying on purpose not to understand. Postnatal depression can only be extended so far. Francesca understands and smiled for the first time today. When she smiled, she seemed like Beatrice, all celestial beatitude.

NOVEMBER 14TH 1979

a.m. Gough Square was only too easy to find and I sat nervously in the LBC lounge waiting to be collected. I regretted my bravado in agreeing to be on live. The producer appeared and introduced himself. I would be on in ten minutes. The programme was called, "Anything Goes." I was taken downstairs into a little room and watched through a glass window the DJ putting on a record. The presenter of my programme arrived and was introduced to me, while the final record of the preceding show played, and ushered me into the next room.

"Hi," he said, "just relax and tell us about your publishing company." I nodded and wondered why I didn't feel nervous. When the record ended and "Anything Goes," was introduced I knew why. I was too frightened to feel anything as mundane as nerves.

"We've got as our first guest Dante Alighieri, who is the managing director of a new publishing company. One which is not the usual publishing venture, as you might guess from its name, DEAD LOSS." He smiled reassuringly at me. "Tell us how you chose such an interesting name Dante?"

"Well what would you call an evening class which started a publishing company, Jim, but DEAD LOSS?"

I laughed at my own joke, as my interviewer smiled bemused.

"Why did your evening class start a publishing company Dante?"

"We're a novel writing class Jim, so obviously publishing is our field."

"But not many writing classes start publishing companies Dante."

"I know Jim, that is why we had to emphasise that fact to get maximum publicity or otherwise people would turn up their noses at our books. Evening class students are supposed to be incompetents in search of competence, not talented novelists."

I drew breath as a whole host of words queued up in my brain ready to get aboard the DEAD LOSS road show.

"Week after week I listened to writing of excellence, certain when the time came it would be published and the class would be a member less. When the time came, the manuscript was returned with the standard rejection letter. Then I would go out and buy a new novel to learn what it had that set it apart from an evening class novel."

"And what did it have Dante?" asked Jim, who seemed anxious to get a word in, "that made it better."

"That's just it Jim, it didn't, most of the novels I read weren't as good. For instance . . ."

Jim shook his head and mouthed the words, "No names Dante."

"For instance," I replied, clearing my throat, "novels about Hampstead and Pimlico in which nothing happened."

"And what happens in your books, Dante?"

"What doesn't Jim, we have it all. The comedy of life from the IRA in the 1920s to modern day problems like baby battering."

"Tell us Dante about the *Comedy*, which is your own novel."

"The *Comedy*," I began, aware now that I couldn't stop. I had the capital's ear and had to fill it with my *Angst* and *Weltpunkt*. I was accelerating like a car going through its gears. There was no lack of words as I had feared but an oversupply, with the only problem to get them all out in the right order.

The waving arms of the producer brought me out of my reverie as the countdown began. The words were being taken out of my mouth. The capital would hear no more.

"Thank you Dante, really great," Jim told me enthusiastically.

I smiled with uncontrollable joy.

"But just one thing Dante."

"Yes Jim?"

"My name is Tom Dante, Jim was the DJ doing the previous programme,"

"Sorry Jim."

The producer enthusiastically sang my praises as he led me upstairs.

p.m. I was too excited to catch the tube home and walked down Fleet Street to Waterloo Bridge. The words which had rushed out in the studio rushed back into my mind. I couldn't have said that, could I? I flinched as I reflected further on my performance, with blind panic replacing euphoria. I had mucked it up. Ten whole minutes of Dante Alighieri gibberish had assaulted the airwaves of the metropolis.

Jim and the producer's praise had just been kindness and politeness as they rushed me out of the studio. I had failed DEAD LOSS and literature with my performance, and even worse Beatrice and Francesca. They would probably be banned from the baby clinic. Sweat accumulated on my brow as I remembered all the people I had told to listen. My parents, the Portinari, the list was endless.

The Thames beckoned invitingly. A noble end after an ignominious life. Bravely I resolved to put an end to it all, after first telephoning Beatrice to have my shame confirmed.

"Did you hear," I asked, hoping against hope that Beatrice had failed to find the frequency on our ancient radio.

"Every word beloved."

"How was I?"

"You sounded just as you always do."

"Was I really that bad?"

"You were great, bighead, and don't start pushing for praise."

"But weren't some of the things I said terrible?"

"They didn't sound like it at this end. You sounded like you had spent all your life doing radio broadcasts."

"I'll be home soon beloved and we can celebrate with champagne."

Happily I was slow in putting the phone down and Beatrice had time to tell me that I was supposed to be meeting her in an hour's time. I had completely forgotten our trip to Manchester. Dante Alighieri took a fond farewell of The Thames, hurrying off to Waterloo underground station. How could I have thought that I had failed and even contemplated pneumonia, as a result of my first attempt to swim without a rubber ring. Beatrice would not lie, would she? Despair and elation fought for control in my mind, with Beatrice holding the scales. Success shone out of her smiling eyes, with Francesca tipping the scales towards a wonderful future.

NOVEMBER 15TH 1979

My radio interviews were prerecorded which was just as well, as a fair bit of editing would be needed to make them worth listening to. I kept talking about death and coffins, despite all the attempts of my interviewers to shift me on to more pleasant subjects. I have concluded that I am better live, my adrenalin working better under pressure.

We waited a half hour in the rain for the photographer from *The Manchester Evening News* who was to accompany

Beatrice, Francesca and I on our repping trip. A nice human interest story, mother and baby in arms helping daddy repping as DEAD LOSS, the evening class which started a publishing company came to Manchester. Well it would have been if he had turned up. Disgruntled and wet we set off repping without our photographer. Sherratt & Hughes, Wilshaws, and Haigh & Hochland succumbed to Beatrice's smiling eyes and Francesca's rather high pitched cries, which daddy could do nothing to lessen.

The highlight of the morning was our trip to the Whitworth Art Gallery, Beatrice feeding Francesca amongst the Impressionists. They made a touching scene, a modern day madonna and child, which proved so attractive to a Japanese tourist that he got his camera out, and took a photo. Before I could protest that my wife and child were not a piece of art to be photographed for his album he was gone, with all the speed of an Olympic athlete. Francesca was obviously upset by this intrusion on her privacy and refused to take any more milk.

Before returning to London we had lunch in the Rajdoot restaurant. Francesca woke up during the main course and despite having a tango with daddy would not stop crying.

"Would you object if my wife breast fed Francesca?" I asked, explaining our problem in the Whitworth Art Gallery. He nodded his approval, his face turning a nice shade of grey under his turquoise turban. We asked for a card when we left promising to be back.

NOVEMBER 16TH 1979

Despite Francesca's nappy which needed changing and Beatrice telling me not to be so silly, I allowed three hours to do a fifteen minute tube journey.

"Better safe than sorry Beatrice," I replied, adamant that no one would say of me that I had been unfortunately delayed in the London traffic when I should have been on the radio talking.

Broadcasting House seemed so large and monumental that I walked around it three times to get its measure before I went in. It was one thing to deliver a press release to it, another to enter as a performer. My confidence was shattered when I introduced myself at the desk and the receptionist told me I was rather early and could I come back in about two hours' time. Pleading hunger I was given a BBC pass and allowed to go upstairs to the staff canteen.

I got excited each time I passed a room of a well known programme. Outside Kaleidoscope I did a three minute homage, dreaming of the day that DEAD LOSS' books would be the talk of Radio 4. My mouth watered outside of Start the Week and PM, as the joy of being interviewed by the superstars of Radio 4 filled my mind.

It was a long but enjoyable walk to the canteen, another 'must' for the BBC tourist. I now know why everyone runs down BBC coffee and food. It is just a ruse to stop the listener feeling jealous, for there would be riots of licence holders outside Broadcasting House if they knew how little things cost. I had five cups of coffee for the price of one in the outside world. As I savoured my low price meal I stared with all the wonderment of a tourist, who is confronting the vistas of his imagination, at the people around me. I tried to tell myself that I was not overawed by sitting in the midst of the famous, in one of the media's greatest shrines, but I failed. One day I would be famous too and belong in places such as this, but for the moment I could not help but feel like the poor cousin up from the country.

Entranced I returned to the reception where I rather self-consciously read (or tried to read) my own book. I got a thrill when someone came and asked for me by name at the desk. My affected modesty disappeared as I heard the man sitting next to me being invited in my stead. Obviously I didn't look like a publisher or an author, while a man old enough to be my father did. He was bald too! When the girl apologised for her error I glared reproachfully at her, getting my revenge. It was another epic walk to the dungeons of Broadcasting House and I relinquished my hold on my anger and became friends with my escort. She endeared herself to me by asking for a copy of my book. I promised to post her one, pooh poohing my generosity and the loss of a sale.

In the room adjacent to the recording room there were coffee and sandwiches for the guests. Despite being bursting at the seams from my subsidized BBC meal upstairs, I politely ate some sandwiches and drank coffee. I was doing exactly what I considered a guest should do, desperately anxious to be invited back.

It was a shock when the interview began, to learn that the programme presenter had actually read my book and was asking serious questions about it. This completely threw me, as I didn't see myself here as Dante Alighieri, the author, but as Dante Alighieri who had started DEAD LOSS; the evening class which had begun a publishing company. There was almost nothing about DEAD LOSS and I felt flattered to be on as an author, as if I was published by a big and serious publisher. If it wasn't for the fact I was really having to concentrate to answer the questions my mind would have floated off in triumph.

I was home in time to hear myself on the radio and nearly fainted when I realised that the braying voice on the air was mine.

"I feel sick Beatrice," I yelled, as I rushed off to the bathroom. Sitting on the loo I tried to think of anything or anyone, rather than what was assaulting the nation's airwaves.

"You can come out now Dante as your bit is finished," Beatrice called out from outside.

The inquest of my first broadcast to the nation was cut short by a phone call from Elizabeth, in a state of drunken hysteria. She was not and never would put herself in a coffin and jump out of it in Covent Garden, whether or not I killed her, as I probably would.

NOVEMBER 17TH 1979

a.m. We parked the van in a side street in Covent Garden. After Yoll had checked the coast was clear, we slid the coffin out of the van, raising it on to our shoulders and made our way nonchalantly to the Piazza. I at least looked serious as the coffin weighed a ton, unlike Yoll who had the giggles in the rear. A crowd of uninvited mourners followed our procession to the large church in Covent Garden. The coffin was laid in front of the entrance and the lid was slowly raised, my beatitude popping out in her black undies screaming:

"What is lost is found, what was dead is alive. DEAD LOSS is here and the novel is reborn."

Jane Austen uncorked the Asti Spumante, and Beatrice drank the first glass. Mary Shelley inundated the bystanders with DEAD LOSS leaflets, while the pallbearers looked around for the tv cameras and throng of newspaper photographers and journalists. A shivering Beatrice pulled on her jeans and sweater, before disappearing in search of Francesca, who was playing nearby with Mrs. Portinari.

"Where was everyone?" asked Mary Shelley, as we sat disconsolately on the coffin drinking sparkling wine.

"I knew the whole business was madness," said Anthony Trollope, "and I was a fool to get myself mixed up in any of it."

At that moment my life's ambition became to kill Anthony Trollope, and I ground my teeth in silent rage.

"I think you can safely say we got gezumped by something better," said Jane Austen, as she refilled the plastic cups with sparkling wine.

We would have probably spent the morning drowning our sorrows in the Piazza if it wasn't for the approach of a policeman, and his invitation to accompany him to Bow Street police station. It seems that there are bye-laws which won't allow you to put a coffin where you like in Covent Garden.

"So much for the English fairplay," I yelled at the policeman as he led us off with the coffin.

In the police station I demanded that we be arrested and charged with an offence, but we were let off with a caution. I'm even a failure as a lawbreaker.

p.m. I rang up all those makers of broken promises to hear the same story.

"Sorry mate everyone was sent out to cover the NGA strike."

It seems that there are no newspapers and so DEAD LOSS is to be born in oblivion. *The Times* article is lost, the Mail. The list is endless. I was feeling really depressed, so I went for a walk down Charing Cross Road to see how our books were selling. Feeling even more depressed I arrived home to see Toni and his little brats watching in open mouthed amazement the arrival of twenty-five thousand books at The Riots.

"The whole house is like a warehouse," Beatrice said as she changed Francesca's nappy on a mattress of books. "We have more books than Brixton Library."

NOVEMBER 18TH 1979

Still no newspapers. The phone hasn't rung once. My father, Mr. Portinari, Giovanni and Pietro come and go as the twenty-five thousand books are moved out to storage.

"Please Dante," my brother Pietro said, "no more books or we'll have to buy a warehouse. There are only so many garages in South London."

Toni spent the day tinkering with his truck, it seems that it recently needs a great deal of attention.

NOVEMBER 19TH 1979

Still no newspapers. The phone rang three times, cancelling my three remaining radio appearances. I would have cried but Beatrice and Francesca were present. I went repping instead to Brighton, even though my heart was not in it. As I told Beatrice, every order reduces a pile of books in someone's garage. Beatrice suggested we should apply for an EEC subsidy for growing books. Like most Florentine women she has no sense of humour.

NOVEMBER 20TH 1979

The invoice for the reprint arrived, to pay it would leave us penniless so I put it under the bed. I tried to ring up Yoll, but his line is permanently unavailable. No one knows about the reprint, not even Beatrice, and I will try and keep it secret for as long as I can. No one will now understand why I reprinted while still having large supplies from the first batch left. I am a failure as a businessman. My destiny it seems is to be a failure.

NOVEMBER 21ST 1979

Wolfgang returned full of orders from Scotland and the North. The whole world will soon have our books gathering dust on their shelves. We sent Wolfgang off up to Stratford for the weekend, so that he can rep Birmingham and the Midlands. The newspapers have returned but there is no mention of us anywhere.

NOVEMBER 22ND 1979

We are mentioned in the business section of both the *Financial Times* and the *Financial Weekly*. We need adventure capital the article said, giving the phone number of The Riots. I did not leave the phone the whole day, and got most excited when it rang at 3 p.m..

"I've read the piece in the *Financial Weekly*."

"Yes," I replied joyfully, thinking all our problems were over.

"And if you're interested I have a novel for you."

"Sorry, a novel?"

"A manuscript for your consideration."

My heart disappeared into my trousers.

"Send it in," I said, "we're always looking for good stuff."

I put the phone down as he was saying thank you. Everyone, it seems, has a novel, even businessmen, but no one has any money to spare. This is at least something I have learnt from my time in publishing.

DECEMBER 1ST 1979

I begin ringing up the literary editors of every newspaper in existence imploring anyone I can get on the other end of the phone to give us a review. It is as if Fleet Street is frightened to review us, just in case they say the wrong thing. I have divided bookpage editors into good guys and bad guys. The good guys are the ones you can get on the other end of the phone and who will at least listen, the bad guys are the ones who are never available. The good guys give you hope by just being there, while the bad guys put you down by making you feel you don't exist.

DECEMBER 2ND 1979

The Guardian suggest I send in another set of review copies, without making any promises that they will fare any better than the first lot. *Time Out* was very sympathetic and said they were thinking about reviewing us in the New Year. This made my day, the idea that someone is thinking of reviewing us acting like a consolation prize for a whole day spent on the telephone.

When I know a few bookmen and can indulge in face to face conversation, I will ask them a question which is intriguing me. Why is it when every editor has fifty plus books a week arriving on his desk, that nearly every newspaper, periodical and magazine, as if by magic, choose the identical half dozen books to review? Is there some kind of book grapevine, or does every editor ring up his opposite number to check that their selection is the correct one? I now look at books in the shops to see if they have "review me" concealed on the cover page.

As the managing director of a publishing company without a review, I take comfort that when we have arrived in the ranks of the obligatory reviewed, the up and coming competition will be kept at bay by the same system. For DEAD LOSS there is only one way to go, and that is up.

DECEMBER 3RD 1979

I had a dream that we had won the Booker Prize and woke up screaming, "We're made, we're made". Unfortunately my dream woke up Francesca and I had to spend the next hour walking her around the room as she wailed her disgust at the Booker Prize judges. All five of our novels were entered, without one being shortlisted. In my dream we came first, second, third and fourth with only Anthony Trollope's novel getting nowhere. Francesca must have had the same dream as she slept with divine reverie, that is until she awoke with the most piercing yelps at 5.30 a.m.

"Just a bad case of The Bookers," I told Beatrice as she got out to comfort our little beloved and give her breakfast. "Yes just a bad case of The Bookers," I repeated. My laughter, Beatrice told me later, soon changing into a rhythmic snore.

Tonight I will dream even better dreams, shunning the Booker for the Nobel. One must be ambitious in one's dreaming.

THE THIRD NOTEBOOK

The Rebirth

DECEMBER 25TH 1979

Giovanni Yerga will save DEAD LOSS, with the help of D. H. Lawrence. Millions of English readers will discover Italy's greatest novelist, thanks to us. Inexplicably Verga is out of print in England, and after long and complicated negotiations we have captured Giovanni Verga from Penguin Books. Even my father thinks it is a good idea and is prepared to advance Italian culture by paying the printing costs for the two Verga books. He will also have a word with my brothers about investing in Verga.

"They owe it," papa said, "to Italy."

I will see if my father feels the same in the new year, when he hasn't a litre of Chianti inside him and Francesca on his knee.

The turkey this year was delicious, probably because it was fed on maize and was imported specially for the occasion from Italy. My parents used up two rolls of film, with nearly all the photos of Francesca on her own. Beatrice thinks this is going too far and if it continues Francesca will grow up thinking she is some kind of superstar.

"She will," said Beatrice, "be bigger headed even than daddy."

DECEMBER 26TH 1979

A long tedious day as the Portinari dote on Francesca, with Beatrice's mother cuddling her incessantly as if she were some kind of doll.

"I won't have it," I told Beatrice in the kitchen, "and if you don't tell your mother to stop, I will."

"Please Dante, shut up, and drink your Chianti," Beatrice said, before giving me a kiss and a very suggestive wink.

"It is unhealthy," I protested, "a grown woman acting that way."

Beatrice stopped smiling and raised her soft melodious voice into a high pitched scream, rather like Francesca's when she's hungry. She told me in Italian to get myself castrated and that if I said another word she would tell her parents to fling the thousands of DEAD LOSS books in their garage onto the streets where they belonged.

I lowered my hands, which I had raised to throttle my beatitude, and said nothing, calming myself by doing the washing up instead. When the Portinari finally left I excelled myself by kissing Mrs. Portinari on both cheeks. Mrs. Portinari excelled herself by embracing me, putting her tongue in my mouth. She kisses just like Beatrice.

I belonged, Beatrice said, in the spare room but as it was Christmas I could share her bed.

DECEMBER 27TH 1979

I reread the D. H. Lawrence translations of *Verga's Mastro Don Gesualdo* and *The Short Sicilian Novels*. They are brilliant, in fact the best thing Lawrence ever wrote and even improve on the excellence of the original. Full of excitement I rang Yoll up. "Giovanni who?" he wanted to know. Mary Shelley was more enthusiastic as she admires Lawrence, but wondered who in England wanted to buy a book from an author, who despite being so brilliant, was unknown even though he died in 1922.

"And Dante," she said, "if he was going to make us rich, why weren't Penguin keeping him, rather than letting him go to DEAD LOSS?"

"Even Penguin make mistakes Mary," I replied, trying to sound confident. Mary Shelley has sown doubts in my mind, but one glance at Beatrice's smiling eyes is enough to overcome them. They are eloquence itself in pleading the case for Verga. Giovanni will triumph of this there can be no doubt! Eventually at least.

DECEMBER 28TH 1979

The board meeting was a success. I feel we are on the right road now. All I have to do is to convince Anthony Trollope to put some effort in and we will get there: DEAD LOSS is still here.

Editor's Note The minutes of the board meeting are in the DEAD LOSS files and are reproduced below.

MINUTES OF THE BOARD MEETING OF DECEMBER 28th 1979.
Those present:

Dante Alighieri
Beatrice Portinari
Yoll
Jane Austen
Mary Shelley

Those not present:

Wolfgang Goethe
Anthony Trollope
Richard Grenville

Apologies for absence:

Wolfgang Goethe
Richard Grenville

1) The Minutes of the first board meeting were taken as read.
2) The Managing Director's Report.
The sales of our first list are slow, with at most twenty per cent of the books out in the bookshops sold. Sales will if anything slow down unless something is done to draw attention to our books and stimulate demand.

Publicity received to date:

A business column piece in *The Financial Times* and *The Financial Weekly*.
A trade piece in *The Bookseller*.
Articles in the *TLS*, *TES* and *South London Press*.
One BBC Radio 2 broadcast, 3 commercial and local BBC radio broadcasts.

Forthcoming:

Radio Hereward and an article in the *Peterborough Evening Telegraph*.

Book reviews:

None so far.

MOTION
That DEAD LOSS tries a relaunch in the New Year in an effort to generate sales.
Motion passed unanimously, with Dante Alighieri nominated to arrange and organise the event.
   3) Company Secretary's Report:
The present finance of the company is as follows:

Balance in current a/c — £12.31
Balance in deposit a/c — NIL
Bills outstanding — NIL
Payments received from bookshops NIL

MOTION
That further investment in DEAD LOSS be encouraged by whatever means.
Motion passed unanimously.
   4) Future Titles:
A list of 32 books was presented to the board by Dante Alighieri as possible titles in a Classics Series. Reservations

were expressed by Yoll, Mary Shelley and Jane Austen as to the commercial strength of the suggested titles and that they were all translations of unknown Italian authors. It is agreed to go ahead with the D. H. Lawrence translations of Verga, the cost of publication to be met by investment by Mr. L. Alighieri, Mr. G. Alighieri and Mr. P. Alighieri.

5) Titles in preparation:

Oberammergau: A Passion Play.

Concern was expressed in the delay in delivering a completed typescript of this work. The February 1st publication date is now impossible and has been put back to April 1st. It was agreed that a letter of censure to Wolfgang Goethe be sent to his last address in America and the project to be cancelled unless a completed manuscript is with the printer by February 1st.

6) Other Business:

It is proposed that Anton Chekov be invited to be the chairman of DEAD LOSS, as an expression of the board of director's appreciation of his advice and help (unpaid). Motion passed unanimously.

That Anthony Trollope be asked to resign from the board. The motion was not put as it was felt that he should be given a chance to vindicate his lack of effort and cooperation with DEAD LOSS and his fellow directors. The Minutes were taken by Jane Austen and are witnessed as being a fair and accurate record of the proceedings.

Editor's Note The letter to Wolfgang Goethe is in the DEAD LOSS files and is reproduced below.

Dear Wolfgang,

Where are you now? And where is the Oberammergau manuscript? Stop chasing round after American girls and return your completed book by the end of the month or otherwise it is too late.

Things are going very badly at the moment and we need all the help we can get. If you want to do anything useful, then visit the major New York publishing houses and sell the rights on the first five books. Someone must want to buy something.

    Yours,

      Dante Alighieri

PS: Francesca sends uncle Wolfgang a big kiss.

PPS: Beatrice asks if you have given up smoking yet?

DECEMBER 31ST 1979

I hope Wolfgang doesn't finish in time as we have no money to pay for his book. If Verga is uncommercial, how much more so must be a Passion Play from a town in Germany, whose name no one can even pronounce let alone have heard of.

Great news, we have had our first payment today. It is a relief to know bookshops actually do pay. I had a nightmare of nobody ever paying until they had sold all the books that they had ordered.

JANUARY 2ND 1980

Rang up *Time Out* who are still thinking about reviewing us, which puts them in a very exclusive group, so exclusive they might end up feeling there is something their best friend won't tell them. While I was on, I asked if they minded if we placed a coffin on their steps on January 15th in aid of DEAD LOSS and its rebirth. They had no objections and even seemed to like the idea. In case they changed their minds I adapted Yoll's press release and hot-footed it up to Media Land and distributed the good news to the waiting hordes. To show my gratitude to *Time Out* I delivered their press release first. Fair, is after all, fair.

January 15th has been selected for a relaunch as it is a quiet time of year in Media Land. I have sent a letter to the NGA begging them not to go on strike on or around that date, sending a copy of my letter to Len Murray at the T.U.C.

JANUARY 3RD 1980

Francesca, Beatrice and I tour the bookshops. That is, Beatrice goes inside and counts how many books have been sold, trying to seem like a book fanatic she puts all our titles face out on the shelves, while Francesca and I freeze outside. The trouble about touring the bookshops is it is depressing. I have added a new proverb to the English language:

"A watched book is a book that doesn't sell."

I have promised Beatrice our tours are at an end and as I lack the courage to present myself in a repping capacity in any bookshop, I have begun writing another novel. It is a sequel to my *Comedy*, and is to be called the *Tragedy*.

JANUARY 4TH 1980

a.m. Wolfgang called from Heathrow Airport. He has had his heart broken in Los Angeles, mended in San Francisco and rebroken in Washington D.C. It was, he said, quite a successful trip. He has translated the play and with my help, he is certain, that the book will be finished on time.

p.m. I met Wolfgang in the British Library Reading Room in Row B. He has twenty-nine books in front of him, all on this unpronounceable town in Germany's Passion Play.

"When we have read these, we can write the introduction," said Wolfgang.

I suggested and got a coffee break. The list shrinks to fifteen over the first cup of coffee and to nine over the second. Unfortunately Wolfgang refuses to drink a third cup. We returned to Row B and select the crucial volumes. I am to do the theatrical and Wolfgang the more serious stuff, it was decided. However, as I can't read German, we changed our plan of campaign. I am now to read the four books in English and Wolfgang the five in German, then each of us will write his own part based on what he has read. The overlap would be edited out.

JANUARY 5TH 1980

2.30 a.m. I have finished reading Wolfgang's translation of the *Oberammergau Passion Play.* I was most impressed by the Play and feel keen to do my part for the book. The play is to be sent up to the printer today, and they have promised the first proofs will be back within a fortnight.

10.30 a.m. Had a huge row with Beatrice for not waking me up at eight o'clock and I was so angry I didn't even kiss my beloved Francesca good-bye. Before beginning work at the British Library Reading Room I eat humble pie, Telecom style. I am forgiven and beam at everyone in Row B, as I begin Chamber's, *The Medieval Stage.* It is great fun reading other people's books so that you can write your own. Cheating really, using other people's ideas as your own and passing yourself off as a so-called expert.

JANUARY 10TH 1980

I have finished my part on Oberammergau and have given it to Beatrice to read. Wolfgang is still in the British Library making notes. Our book must have depth, he says, it is not after all a novel. I ignore the intended slight, saying readability is the key, not gravity nor profundity. Having got involved in the project I feel it is up to me to keep Wolfgang on the rails. I've given him a week to finish, threatening to produce the book without his sections otherwise.

JANUARY 11TH 1980

a.m. Beatrice says my introduction is boring and reads like someone else wrote it. She is however enthusiastic about the book. I must, she says, rewrite my piece in my own words.

p.m. I rewrite my thirty-five pages until they become a tight twenty-two. It is a lot better, the next draft, Beatrice says, should be perfect. There is not, I replied angrily, going to be third draft, and I register my protest at this veiled criticism by refusing to change Francesca's nappy.

When Wolfgang returned from the British Library at 6.30, I gave him my piece to read.

JANUARY 12TH 1980

a.m. We had our first returns today. I refused to be depressed, taking comfort in the six books sold, rather than worrying about the nineteen returned.

Before departing for the British Library Wolfgang gave me his critique on my Oberammergau introduction.

"It was good," he felt, "but lacking in grammar. You cannot," he said, "write about the Middle Ages in the present tense. And Dante, sentences must have commas and proper punctuation."

I am now writing about Wolfgang Goethe in the past tense. The world seems to be going crazy when a German feels competent to teach an Italian English grammar. I have put Wolfgang's list of inappropriate expressions and words down the loo with Francesca's dirty nappy.

p.m. I rewrite the Oberammergau introduction. It has now only fifteen pages and is written in the past tense, with every sentence crawling with commas. Beatrice has given her approval. Beatrice spends Francesca's sleep periods ringing up Media Land. Her soft melodious voice coaxing even the reticent to attend the rebirth of DEAD LOSS. When I telephone, I appeal to my listener's guilt complex, describing how it feels to sit media-less with a coffin in Covent Garden. Everyone says they are coming. Perhaps this time it's second time lucky.

JANUARY 13TH 1980

A girl rang up for a job. She thought we were pretty cool and wrote the most far out press releases she had ever put in the waste paper basket. I explained that there were no jobs of the paid sort going, but there was work in abundance of the voluntary variety. She could even take part in our stunt, and spend the afternoon drinking champagne. It is, she says, her scene, and she'll be round tomorrow for an interview.

Anthony Trollope rang in. He has had a change of heart and wants to be a pallbearer. He did not mention Mary Shelley's phone call, telling him of the BBC and ITV cameras coming.

There is nothing like appearing on television to induce a change of heart.

JANUARY 14TH 1980

Our new "do anything" member of the DEAD LOSS collective has bright green hair splayed out like peacock feathers. Her clothes matched her hair in multicoloured splendour. She didn't take any persuading to be our stunt girl and freaked out with joy en route to Covent Garden for the rehearsal. She almost bounced into the coffin when the time came, not even objecting when the lid was put on.

As we carried her down Southampton Street I felt happy that we could save the model's hire fee tomorrow. With a bump we lowered the coffin onto the steps of *Time Out* and with theatrical slowness raised the lid. Our "do anything" girl bounced out, screaming, her green hair prematurely grey, as she sprinted away towards The Strand.

"Oh well," said Yoll, "she was not really our kind of girl, although she had a certain potential."

Beatrice was put on standby duty when we got home, but despite the five supplicant authors on their knees in front of her, she refused to change her mind.

JANUARY 14TH 1980

a.m. The great day had arrived and The Riots became a real hot bed of activity. The hearse arrived at ten o'clock, dead on time, and we all piled in to be driven to our celebratory breakfast at Jacaranda Garden. Upstairs we drank our own sparkling wine, over Jacaranda's bacon and eggs.

It was a jolly DEAD LOSS collective that piled into the hearse, waving and hiccupping at the passers-by. Wolfgang even screamed out of the window:

"It is only a novel which is dead, but don't worry it will be coming alive again at eleven o'clock."

We arrived at Covent Garden and parked on a double yellow line. It didn't take long to find our model, she was walking up and down Southampton Street in a distraught state. It took me a good ten minutes to persuade Gloria that the whole business was not an elaborate practical joke and even longer that she would not be asphyxiated. The doubling of her fee showed we were serious and payment in advance managed to calm her nerves. As promised we only put the lid on the coffin when the hearse entered Southampton Street.

"Further on," yelled Wolfgang, as Mary Shelley stopped the hearse at the Covent Garden end of the street.

"Can't you see the tv cameras Wolfgang?" asked Mary Shelley as she inched the hearse forward towards the YMCA shop.

The high-spirited pallbearers became very serious as they looked down the street at the two lines of photographers, tv cameras and hordes of bystanders. There were even policemen to keep the crowd under control.

"My God this is exciting," said Wolfgang, as the coffin was raised high upon our shoulders.

I bit my lip, trying not to laugh or cry, I wasn't sure which, as I stared at the posse of cameras in front of me, retreating down the street before our cortege. My shoulder felt like giving way as the coffin got heavier at every step. Beatrice waved as we passed her on the street, Francesca gurgling at her daddy as he passed.

We had to wait for what seemed like an eternity for a space to be cleared for us on the steps of *Time Out*. The coffin was lowered with greater care than the night before onto the steps. The lid was slowly removed. Silence decended as nothing happened.

"I bid the novel be reborn and take its rightful place in English life," said Yoll, a trifle too joyfully, for what after all was a tragic Shakespearean cameo of rebirth.

"She rises," screamed the cohorts of the DEAD LOSS, as Gloria arose slowly in her DEAD LOSS colours and black silk leotard. The photographers clicked and clicked. Mary and Jane popped the champagne.

Those eleven minutes of filming were thirsty work, with seventeen bottles of sparkling wine being emptied by the hardworking representatives of the media. The remaining three lasted the best part of an hour when the celebrations continued inside with some of the office staff of *Time Out*. Mary Shelley was lucky not to have got a ticket for the illegal parking of a hearse in Southampton Street, followed by a court appearance for being drunk and disorderly while in charge of a hearse.

The celebrations continued back at The Riots, with white wine replacing the bubbly. It took the caller from *20th Century Fox* a good five minutes before anyone could believe the call was not a hoax. The idea that anyone could even think of making a film of his novel got Anthony Trollope beside himself with euphoria, while it had a sobering effect on his fellow authors.

p.m. Very drunk and exceedingly happy I went off repping, wanting to maximise the avalanche of publicity which was

sure to come, into large book sales. I was irresistible that afternoon, even getting a pet shop to take our books.

We were on for almost two minutes on BBC TV, and a
minute and a half on ITV, both at peak times. Cloud nine
descended and stayed at The Riots, Brixton, with Beatrice
and I making love in a way which transcended all description.
I had nearly forgotten the delights of Beatrice Portinari's body.
The postnatal depression, I think is at an end.

If I was Julius Caesar, I would start the year from January
15th, day one in the DEAD LOSS calendar. Wolfgang
Goethe is a really great babysitter, and walked Francesca round
for hours to get rid of her hiccups while I and Beatrice were
otherwise engaged.

JANUARY 16TH 1980

We appeared pictorially in seven newspapers and were
mentioned in four others. Wolfgang who was supposed to
be writing his Oberammergau piece, spent the day collating
the press cuttings and — when he thought we couldn't hear
— ringing Germany to tell his mother that he was famous.
I don't blame Wolfgang entirely for his forty minute phone
call to his mother in Berchtesgaden, as I think the oversized
adverts plastered over the walls of every tube station, telling
foreign tourists to ring home, must take their share of the
blame. And I will tell British Telecom that when I deduct half
the cost of the phone call from our next bill.

JANUARY 17TH 1980

I'm sure Toni must have seen us on television as he goes green
every time he sets eyes on me. He even tried smiling at us
when we were walking down the road with Francesca, but
we looked the other way. The Alighieri do not exchange
smiles with people who put holes in their roof. Toni as a
Sicilian should understand that. The parish priest has offered

to mediate in what he termed "our dispute". Beatrice's reply was, we would prefer talking to the devil than a Sicilian with a hammer in his hand. The priest who is from Palermo smiled before going next door to Toni and his five members of the junior Mafia.

We are still waiting for some kind of response from the stunt. No one had even asked for my autograph.

JANUARY 18TH 1980

Wolfgang's sixty-five pages on Oberammergau reads like a bad translation from a 19th century German text book which got remaindered the the day after it was published. "We can't publish this," I told Wolfgang, whose eyes glared back, "why not?" "It is too heavy Wolfgang, with too much of everything — facts, dates and incidents."

"You tell me this, you who have no grammar and no tenses?"

I nodded as a furious Wolfgang stormed out. In his absence I cut his sixty-five pages down to nineteen. On his return for lunch, Wolfgang was struck speechless by my act of vandalism. He ate his potato soup in silence, before going to the spare room to pack his suitcase. After kissing Beatrice and Francesca good-bye he left.

"I am going to Germany, Dante Alighieri, where learning is appreciated and art understood. My manuscript is a work of culture which will find a German publisher."

It is lonely being a publisher. Your authors hate you and the general public try to ignore your existence.

JANUARY 21ST 1980

It was a very good morning. We received nine orders and eleven payments in the post. It made me feel like the managing director of a real publishing company. But if I were, I would have an office somewhere and be denied the pleasure of coming down for breakfast and finding my nine orders and eleven payments. There was even a request from Sinn Fein for a review copy of Anthony Trollope's *Ireland and Enfields Green*. I thought that a nerve, and said that they should pay for their copy like everyone else. Beatrice persuaded me otherwise, saying it might be dangerous to refuse. I enclosed a compliment slip with the book, thanking Sinn Fein for their interest in DEAD LOSS. We celebrated DEAD LOSS' best ever post by having a hearty English breakfast. Francesca had her usual baby gunge, but seemed to realize that it was a special occasion by having a second tin.

Foolhardy after such a good start to the day I made my way to the Penguin Bookshop in Covent Garden. My heart missed a beat when I couldn't find a single copy of any of our books on the shelves. We had sold out! Cock-a-hoop I sought out the blonde hair and blue eyes of my baked bean purchaser, demanding a repeat order. Despite trying with all my might, I couldn't refrain from gloating all over my publisher's face.

"I'm afraid not Mr. DEAD LOSS. What we have for you are these."

I opened the nicely packed bundle, finding twenty-four books.

"We managed to sell one copy of *Ireland and Enfields Green*, and that's all I'm afraid. Please credit us for the rest."

"But we've been on TV and in the papers."

"Yes I know, but you haven't sold any books."

My plans for a day spent repping gave way to a consolation drink or two in most of Covent Garden's many wine bars. I was perplexed, if TV and newspapers articles could not sell our books, what could? Publishing, I concluded, was a decidedly difficult business.

JANUARY 22ND 1980

There were five orders and five payments today. We were going forward. I rang round the cohorts of the DEAD LOSS to see who would be available to do some repping next month.

Everyone seemed to be otherwise engaged. It appears Fate has declared that it will have to be Dante Alighieri doing a lone stint with only *Mastro Don Gesualdo* to keep him company.

The Oberammergau cover arrived with the final proofs and is a stunner. I sent a copy to Wolfgang over the water as a peace offering, with a little note attached. It read: "Come home super rep, we need you."

JANUARY 26TH 1980

There was no post today whatsoever. It is the first day since DEAD LOSS started that we have failed to receive something through the letterbox of The Riots. I was cheered up, in the afternoon, by the arrival of four thousand copies of *Mastro Don Gesualdo*. I took a few copies round to my father and brothers, so that they could see what their money had bought. The books are for the moment to be stored in our hall. It shouldn't take long to sell the first batch and get into a reprint.

"Giovanni Verga will make us rich," I told Beatrice and Francesca, who both smiled sharing my confidence in Giovanni.

JANUARY 27TH 1980

The post today consisted of a circular and a begging letter from an organisation which purported to represent the National Libraries of Scotland and Wales, and the Libraries of Oxford, Cambridge and Trinity College, Dublin, demanding five free copies of each of our books. It seems that there is no end to the organisations who expect to get something for nothing. The next time I want a book, I will write off for a review copy.

FEBRUARY 1ST 1980

The repping is going well for *Mastro* and the forthcoming Oberammergau book. If it weren't for the fact that a lot of the orders are contingent on taking back the first five books, business would be booming. My father now has a rotating bookstand in his delicatessen, selling our books. So there is at least one shop which won't ask to send any books back.

When I got home, I had a nice surprise waiting for me: seventeen pages on Oberammergau from Wolfgang. He had enclosed a note. It read:

"How is your grammar these days?"

FEBRUARY 2ND 1980

There was one repeat order in the post this morning, for *Ireland and Enfields Green*. Our rep from Northern Ireland wrote to tender his resignation. This was a shock as I had forgotten that we had one there. The two orders he had managed to obtain for us lead me to believe that he won't be any great loss.

At the Art Centre, the five members of the DEAD LOSS collective, spent a cheerful evening discussing our future.

"What we need?" says Mary Shelley, "are reviews, or otherwise we're sunk."

"We're sunk anyway," commented Anthony Trollope, before going off home, it being his round.

Undeterred by our neglect in the Land of the Media, we resolve to send out another set of review copies. For whatever else it did, it at least reduced our stock of unsold books.

FEBRUARY 3RD 1980

Rang round Media Land begging for reviews. I had six non-availables, one, "I'm too busy to talk," and two sympathetic nos. I lacked the courage to ring up *Time Out*, who were in the process of reviewing us, just in case they changed their minds. The man who was reviewing us there, seemed to like a long time to meditate before putting pen to paper.

Although somewhat downcast I went out repping in the afternoon. I felt I owed it to Giovanni Verga, Italy's greatest novelist.

FEBRUARY 4TH 1980

Beatrice and I had a long and serious chat about our future.

"There must come a time, when we say, enough is enough," said Beatrice, "and that you get a proper job."

I had been waiting for this conversation and despite trying to encourage Beatrice with the great things that the future held for us, felt somewhat discouraged myself.

"We can't live on air Dante," Beatrice told me, as Francesca slept peacefully in her cot. "If DEAD LOSS can't pay its way. . . ."

FEBRUARY 5TH 1980

Went repping more determined than ever that we would succeed. I was repping the outer suburbs, so needed all my determination. There is little enthusiasm for small publishers the further you get away from the city centre. I packed up at three p.m., having only repped a half dozen books. On the way home I called in to see my parents in the delicatessen. While my father was slicing salami I inquired if he had any part time work going. Papa said he and mama could manage, and Mrs. Spinosa still came in on Saturdays. I don't think he realised I was asking for work for me and I felt too embarrassed to make it clear.

FEBRUARY 10TH 1980

George, a pal of mine from my pupillage days came to lunch. He thought DEAD LOSS was a great success as our books are in every bookshop he's been in. Beatrice and I smiled at his innocence. I knew I should tell him that we are still in all the bookshops as our books don't sell, and that any day now will be on their way home with a Return Note. Instead I changed the subject and asked George how it felt to be a successful Junior Counsel? I must have said the wrong thing as he immediately changed the subject back to publishing.

I slept very badly as Francesca is teething and can't sleep. At one stage I dreamt that I was being buried surrounded by Return Notes, and the soil wasn't dirt, but thirty thousand burgundy books. As I was being lowered in I woke up screaming. Beatrice says if I keep on having nightmares, I will have to sleep in the spare room. It is the third time this week.

FEBRUARY 14TH 1980

I encountered a friend of mine in Dillons, and tried to persuade him to buy a copy of each of our books. He seemed rather dubious, so I resorted to moral blackmail, saying friendship was surely worth £2.50. His reply was that he felt that friendship at that price was somewhat overpriced and in this particular instance was only worth £1.95. Slightly dismayed I bought a copy of my *Comedy*, and gave it to him. At least showing that for me friendship was worth £2.50.

In the afternoon we celebrated St.Valentine's Day by a trip to the zoo at Regents Park. Francesca, for some reason decided to sleep through everything, including the chimpanzee's Tea Party. I find the zoo relaxing, as it reminds me that there are others worse off than we are.

FEBRUARY 15TH—17TH 1980

I took Beatrice and Francesca away for a few days. We had a really nice time in York. The low point was an overpriced pseudo French meal which was just yuck, and not the big treat I intended it to be. Beatrice's postnatal depression seems definitely to be over, as she didn't protest when I said we might as well rep the bookshops while we were here.

She did however put her foot down on the way home, when I suggested we broke our journey at Peterborough, so that I could rep Webster's Bookshop. Poor Webster's, they must remain, at least for the moment DEAD LOSS–less. But as they don't know we exist, they shouldn't mind too much.

FEBRUARY 18TH 1980

I had a tremendous shock while I was out repping. The town with the unpronounceable name, that no one has ever heard of, with its Passion Play, had three books about it on the bookshelves. I could kill Wolfgang Goethe and his: "We are fulfilling a great need. People want books on Oberammergau, but there are simply none available."

Down the road when I tried to rep Oberammergau I was told:

"Ober –whatsitsname? Sorry mate, never heard of it."

And I burst out laughing, telling my never-heard-of-it mate about the bookshop down the road. He seemed somewhat shamefaced and said he would give it a try and took three.

"We are," I told him, "the only ones with the complete text in English."

He thought for a little, then changed the three to five.

The second shock was how slowly *Mastro Don Gesualdo* seems to be selling. Perhaps I was naive to expect bookshops to sell out within a month, but it came as an unexpected blow to see the ordered copies gathering dust on the shelves. The English, it seems, are incapable of appreciating great literature; and great literature from Italy seems doubly unacceptable. Take note English illiterati, your standards are under attack and will be changed by us. DEAD LOSS, Verga, Literature and Italy will prevail.

FEBRUARY 19TH 1980

a.m. I was just ready, after our Italian breakfast of black coffee and biscuits, to go out into the cold and rep when we had a caller. It was a Mr. Fashing from, You've got it, We remainder it Ltd., who was very keen to buy our books, even the recently arrived copies of *Mastro Don Gesualdo*. He was like a dream made flesh. Six thousand copies of a modern novel, he would take, regardless of quality.

When he mentioned his price of 10p a book, my smile soured to a gargoyle grin.

"We give," I said, "thirty-five percent, sometimes under duress forty per cent, and fifty per cent to wholesalers, but as of present, we do not offer ninety-five percent discounts to anyone."

I didn't exactly throw him out, but it was very clear that he was unwelcome and he left in great haste, the Alighieri once roused are dangerous to behold. Toni and his little brood of truants saw him out.

p.m. Depressed by, You've got it, We remainder it Ltd., I stayed at home, ringing Media men. During one of my rest periods I went for a walk in the garden and found it full of next door's rent-a-brats, who disappeared over the wall on my approach. That was it. I rushed round and knocked at Toni's door. He was out, so I told Mrs. Toni, if I saw the rent-a-brats in my garden again, they would have my writ the next day.

FEBRUARY 20TH 1980

a.m. The second Verga book arrived. Toni was supervising its arrival until I went outside to talk about his kids. He got in a huff and walked off, and pretended not to hear, when I said, if he put any more holes in my roof, the police would be round to arrest him. The neighbours, Britain's evergrowing multitude of unemployed, heard and smirked behind their net curtains. No one likes Toni and his rent-a-brats, with the possible exception of Mrs. Toni Rent-a-brats.

I moved the two Verga books to the spare room.

p.m. Wolfgang arived unannounced from Germany. We embraced fraternally. While he was playing with Francesca,

Beatrice and I prepared his next UK holiday. He would rep Scotland via Birmingham and Manchester. We included a few free days in his schedule for sightseeing in The Trossacks. When I gave him the agreed itinerary he presented me with a new list of ungrammatical expressions and usages which he wanted deleted from my part of the Oberammergau introduction. Wolfgang, I told him, if it's possible we will get William Caxton to incorporate your changes.

I rang Mr. Caxton in front of Wolfgang and was relieved to hear the book was printed and at the binders. Wolfgang was thrilled and dismayed simultaneously at this news. We changed Wolfgang's schedule so he could pick up some car stock at Gloucester en route. Gloucester we assured him was an historic town.

FEBRUARY 22ND 1980

The spare room sleeps Wolfgang, eight thousand books in English by Giovanni Verga and is DEAD LOSS' office, containing the only telephone in the house. It is not a satisfactory situation. We need, said Wolfgang, a larger house. Every time he gets up to go to the loo in the night he bumps into Giovanni Verga. Like most Germans, Wolfgang for some reason, seems to dislike Italians, even dead ones, although professing a love of Italy. A German dream is obviously an Italy without Italians.

Beatrice counts the days until Wolfgang leaves and she can fumigate the spare room.

FEBRUARY 25TH 1980

I had a nightmare last night. Giovanni Verga got out of his coffin and laughed at me, standing next to the bed, saying:

"Only an Alighieri would be so stupid as to publish my books in England."

I was worried that in my dream Verga spoke English, for as far as I know Verga spoke no English, although he once visited London with Luigi Capuana. The imagination plays strange tricks on the overwrought sensibilities of a small publisher.

Happily Wolfgang left for his repping mission and the spare room can be fumigated. All Francesca's baby grows smell of uncle Wolfgang's nicotine. Beatrice has declared The Riots a non-nuclear and non-smoking zone. Wolfgang is a member of Green Peace and a supporter of the GLC and smokes fifty cigarettes a day. He will resist, I told Beatrice, this restriction on his liberty.

"Then he can stay up in The Highlands and smoke Scotland to death."

Francesca is teething again.

MARCH 1ST 1980

When Wolfgang rang up to give his progress report I couldn't help but interrupt him.

"We've been reviewed Wolfgang," I screamed joyfully down the phone, "we have been reviewed."

The line went dead shortly afterwards, Wolfgang obviously fainted from shock at this unexpected good news. When he rang back two hours later I outlined the stupendous happenings of the week. *Time Out*, true to it's promise, had reviewed us on the same day that *City Limits* had.

"It is, as I've said, Wolfgang," I blurted out, full of British Telecom rapture, "when one does another does. It is as if there is an unwritten law, if your opposite number does you have to. There is no choice."

I continued ecstatically outlining my theory on being reviewed until Wolfgang reminded me he was paying for this call and would have to ring off.

I had nobly omitted to tell Wolfgang that *Time Out* for some reason had not reviewed my book, and *City Limits* had done likewise, also excluding Mary Shelley's *Frankenstein*, from their review page. It seems the *Comedy* and vampires are out of fashion, or as I suspect in my case, pushy publishers who are always on the phone using up the review editor's precious time must take the consequences. I am now the only member of DEAD LOSS without a review. I who founded the collective, do all the work (pace Beatrice) and appeared on the radio, am considered unworthy of a review. It reinforces my destiny: Dante Alighieri was born to be a publisher and not an author. For some strange reason, *Time Out* and *City Limits* think Anthony Trollope is a genius. I write, "Anthony Trollope is a genius", up on the message's board, as who am I to disagree with the critics?

Beatrice's aversion to Anthony Trollope seems to be growing.

MARCH 3RD 1980

a.m. I tried the literary magazines and *The Guardian* again, delivering the review copies in person of our "reviewed books". By eleven o'clock I was back home, ringing the editors up pleading our case. Three promised a review, two were unavailable and two said we had missed the boat.

Anthony Trollope rang inviting me to a celebratory DEAD LOSS party. I felt like declining his invitation, but as the party is to take place at the office, it would be hard not to be present. Success has gone to Anthony Trollope's head in a big way. He has, he said, begun his second novel. So sure of its success, he has taken a month off work, unpaid, to write it in. I felt like telling him to wait until people started buying his first book, but didn't as that would sound like sour grapes from an "unreviewed" author.

Beatrice is furious that we are having a DEAD LOSS party at The Riots, as in her opinion we haven't anything to celebrate.

"When we sell some books," she said, "then it will be the time to celebrate."

Beatrice reminded me of her parents' car which would like to get back into its garage. I told Beatrice, in my defence, that the party was not my idea, which made her even angrier and if she had known Anthony Trollope's phone number she would have Telecommed him to pieces.

p.m. To appease Beatrice and to get out of changing Francesca's nappy I went out repping, trying to get some of the bookshops who returned the first five books to take them back, at least the reviewed titles.

"I will not rest," I assured Beatrice, "until every DEAD LOSS book is out of your parents' garage and their BMW is back inside, snug and warm once again."

I began at Penguin's Covent Garden Bookshop, having tanked up with red wine en route. When I tracked down the manageress I presented her with a photostat of the *Time Out* and *City Limits* reviews. She read them, nodding her approval.

"I'm glad for you," she said with a smile, returning the photostat.

"Ten of each?" I asked, becoming confident of success.

"But we've had them before and they didn't sell."

Aghast I replied, "I know, but we had no publicity then, it is different now."

"If I took back every title that had had a belated good review we would have no room in the shop for anything else. We've taken your Verga books, Mr. Alighieri, and Oberammergau, as well, so in the circumstances we have been very fair."

"But they will sell now," I objected.

"That may well be, but not here I'm afraid Mr. Alighieri."

"You are a hard woman," I replied defeated.

"Where this shop is concerned I am."

I looked enviously at Covent Garden's many wine bars and it was with tremendous resolve that I managed to steer my way through them to Covent Garden Tube Station. My two bags full of DEAD LOSS books felt unbearably heavy, but I pushed on, remembering the Portinari's BMW out in the cold. What I needed was orders and not red wine, I kept repeating on the tube, aware that at three p.m. my dilemma would be over.

When I got home at six-thirty, I flopped exhausted into the armchair, having got rid of one hundred books. Beatrice rewarded me with a kiss, saying if I kept it up for three more weeks the BMW would just about squeeze in the garage. Beatrice, like all women is never satisfied.

Wolfgang rang in from Poulde-le-Fylde, a town which sounds like it should be in Scotland, but is, he assures me, in Lancashire. He is in love and has been so for four days. He met an American student from Yale in the Trossacks and they are now together in Lancashire. Wolfgang put my mind at ease by saying Brenda thinks DEAD LOSS is over the moon, and goes repping with him. Tomorrow they are off to Oxford, before Cambridge, Norwich and London.

Before he put the phone down Wolfgang asked if we could get a double bed for the spare room and move Giovanni out into the hall, and tidy the room up a bit for him and Brenda. It doesn't do, Wolfgang thinks, to create a bad impression at the beginning of a relationship. Beatrice doesn't approve, thinking Brenda might prove a bad influence on Francesca.

"The next time Wolfgang rings, ask him," said Beatrice, "if she smokes? And if she does, tell him that in his absence The Riots has become a smokeless zone. Strictly for non-smokers."

MARCH 7TH—8TH 1980

Before the drinks party we had an editorial meeting, during which we discussed future titles. It was agreed that we would press ahead with books by Pirandello and Grazia Deledda, as they had both won the Nobel Prize for Literature, even though no one, excepting Beatrice and myself, had ever heard of Grazia Deledda or knew that Pirandello was a novelist of high literary merit. To gain the acceptance of Deledda and Pirandello it was agreed to publish two more novels from our writing class. Despite my objections that new fiction was too difficult an area for DEAD LOSS, the majority of the editorial board took the view that the recent reviews had changed that.

After the editorial meeting we convened a board meeting and ratified the decisions of the earlier meeting, before the party began. None of the Media men invited turned up, but it was a jolly boozy affair which was greatly enjoyed by the minor literati present. It was taped by Yoll, who thinks we should send it with our compliments to the Media men who missed the party, so that they would know what they had missed.

I don't know if it was the curry or the wine, but my stomach gave way during the night, and I groaned and roamed about the house begging to be put out of my misery. Beatrice somehow managed to sleep through my hyperacidic agonies, having taken the precaution of putting cotton wool in both her ears before going to bed.

When my sufferings were at their height I wrote out my will leaving everything to Beatrice, except my DEAD LOSS shares, which I bequeathed to the Nation. Francesca slept through the night, so I didn't have even my beloved's gurgles to keep me company.

When the doctor came, I was given the usual prescription and told not to eat curry, fry ups or drink any alcohol.

"Under alcohol," I asked, "do you include wine?"

The doctor nodded in the affirmative, causing me to burst into painful laughter.

"Doctor I'm Italian, not to drink wine for me, is like a day without sunshine. Please don't prescribe for me British remedies."

The doctor's face wore that, "you have been warned look", that GPs must learn as a compulsory subject at college. Making a supreme effort I went the whole day without a glass of wine. I also refused all food, as I couldn't see the point of eating without pleasure.

Not that much came from the *Time Out* and *City Limits* reviews; three orders and perhaps a few dozen extra copies sold in the bookshops. But I'm not disappointed and have written off the first five books as a dead loss. It is only patriotism which stops me writing off Giovanni Verga as well and the hope that the English book buying public will eventually come to its senses. Perhaps I should launch a, "Read a foreign book a day", campaign, or "A Verga book a day keeps boredom away".

But it is all in DEAD LOSS' unsuccessful past. We are, thank heavens, a success, and not before time. The gentle trickle had turned into a flood. Every post bringing an ever-increasing supply of orders, all for this book about the town in Bavaria with the unpronounceable name and its decennial Passion Play.

Publishing of non-fiction is so easy; it is fiction publishing which separates the men from the boys. Having thought about it I think I prefer to be a boy and make money. I'm sure I've grown a full inch in the last few days and I know that every eye turns as I walk down the street.

Verga will soon be lonely in the spare room, the rate that Oberammergau is going out. No need even to rep, the orders come in on their own, through teleordering. I have already ordered another five thousand copies, it would have been twenty thousand but the printer says he couldn't cope with such a large order on such short notice. Brenda and Wolfgang pack in the morning, while I with my elastic arms deliver the central London orders by tube. After lunch Wolfgang and Brenda take the parcels to the Post Office, while Beatrice and I pack. In the evening, on alternate days my parents and the Portinari come to do the packing while Wolfgang and I spend the evening typing out the orders.

In ten days we have dispatched over five thousand books on Oberammergau. The postage bill is horrific. Everything is, as I always knew it would be one day, wonderful. The other DEAD LOSS are permanently unavailable for packing duties. It seems that packing books is not a literary activity, especially when the books to be packed have been written by someone else. But I don't mind as we are a success! The Alighieri wear one big collective smile.

MARCH 28TH 1980

Things are quiet in The Riots now. The orders are still flowing in, but there are no books to flow out. The first seven thousand have gone out (I didn't tell Wolfgang that I tried unsuccessfully to reduce the first print run to two thousand) and the next five thousand have yet to arrive. Wolfgang and Brenda have gone to Germany. They are, as Wolfgang said, in love. Wolfgang, as Beatrice told Brenda during a late night packing session, makes a habit of falling in love.

"I've got the picture, honey," was Brenda's reply.

Wolfgang is repping the book round his native land with his usual fervour. En route to Germany he fixed up a deal for ten thousand copies of the Oberammergau book at wholesale rates to a large tour operator, called Travel Co.

Life is going from wonderful to marvellous in big easy leaps. The books for Travel Co are going straight from the printer to Travel Co's London office. We don't even have to pack them or even set our eyes on them. I have given the printer the go ahead for the Pirandello and Deledda books, with the new fiction to follow when he has time.

APRIL 4TH 1980

Brenda has arrived back at The Riots without Wolfgang, who, it seems, is in love elsewhere. There isn't enough packing to keep her busy, so we have employed Brenda as Francesca's au pair. Brenda is a brilliant nappy changer, and Wolfgang could do a lot worse, I told Beatrice during my nappy changing lesson. Beatrice smiled and said there was more to marriage than changing nappies. Wolfgang, she said, was very German.

APRIL 6TH 1980

An amazing occurrence; we have gone two whole days without an order in the post. I have a terrible thought that everyone who wants a copy of Oberammergau has now bought one. I think of the ten thousand copies sold on sale or return to Travel Co., the three thousand sitting in the spare room, and the five thousand at the binders. Refusing to panic I put an advert in all the religious newspapers, exhorting the faithful to buy. I went out repping again this afternoon, to the East End of London, and managed only to sell seven books. The profit on which isn't enough to pay my tube fare.

APRIL 10TH 1980

I had a phone call from Wolfgang who has started touring already. He has, he said, a job for me doing tours to Oberammergau with Americans for four months. I could sell at least fifty books a week. I got very excited about all the books I could sell and accepted the job, writing off to confirm my acceptance that very afternoon.

Holding Francesca on my knee as Beatrice tries unsuccessfully to get a mouthful of gunge into her closed mouth I felt really guilty. I will never have the courage to tell my little family that I am going to leave them for four whole months during the Summer. Beatrice will never forgive me and I can see that I will spend the rest of my life in the spare room. Poor Francesca already doomed to be an only child.

APRIL 15TH 1980

I had a real shock while I was out repping. Everyone kept ordering copies of, *Ireland and Enfields Green*, and Jane Austen's *Baby Batterers*. I was too pleased to ask anyone why; it made a pleasant change from having them returned. It was only when I got to the Compendium Bookshop that

I found out why. DEAD LOSS' first list was being reborn yet again. We were in *The Guardian*.

My eyes popped out with joy as I read the review. It was official: Anthony Trollope is a genius and Jane Austen was weighty and serious. We were made, yet again! I casually discussed Anthony Trollope and Tolstoy for a few minutes with the buyer before I left. When I was out of sight of the shop, I ran with delirious joy down Camden High Street screaming at the top of my voice: "Eureka, Eureka." The phone box was out of action but the one next to it, which was bathed in urine, was working. I rang Beatrice and when my darling answered, I told her to keep calm and get *The Guardian*.

"Page nine Beatrice, have you got it," I paused, my heart pounding from my first ever five minute mile. "Read the first book review."

Beatrice's heavenly melody embraced the newsprint until it soared into the Alighieri paradise. Each word followed joyfully its fellow, singing the praise of this important new novelist.

"Now the last review Beatrice."

How can I express what it feels like to see your first Fleet Street review and to know that you are after all a publisher and not an imposter. To have been neglected, scorned and passed over, as if unclean, then to be made whole, with a suddenness which was overwhelming. I could not think of anything but that I had to get home to Beatrice and Francesca and celebrate.

On the tube I gurgled like Francesca, my eyes glazed with demented joy, as I rubbed my hands together in uncontrollable glee. The compartment, which was full, emptied, most people going into the next carriage. Left alone with my joy, I walked up and down giggling to myself. At Brixton tube station there were Beatrice and Francesca waiting for me. I was so overjoyed I kissed Brenda as well, the Alighieri love so great that it could embrace all, overflowing into the universe.

That night I spoke with a drunken Anthony Trollope over the phone.

"I am a genius Dante, I am a genius. I always thought I might be, but now ... now there is no doubt. Good-bye Dante, good-bye."

The bottle of champagne I had bought for the editor of *The Guardian* book page, which was already gift wrapped, proved too tempting, and was drunk at midnight.

"Sorry Bill, our need was too great!"

APRIL 16TH 1980

My head is not on speaking terms with the rest of my body and I spent a very quiet day in bed. Beatrice, or perhaps its Brenda, floats round my bed like an angel administering tonics.

My resolution for April is to learn how to drink like a successful publisher. Just keep the reviews rolling in and I'll get there.

APRIL 17TH 1980

As *The Guardian* has reviewed us it is now time for *The Times* to do likewise and so I sent off another review copy with a copy of *The Guardian* review. What *The Guardian* had done today, *The Times* will do tomorrow. My theory about reconciable opposites seems to be foolproof. I say my, but it is not exactly original, and I admit I got it from James Joyce's *Finnegans Wake*, and Joyce got it from Giordano Bruno. As far as I know Giordano Bruno has kept very quiet on where he obtained it from.

APRIL 21ST 1980

Francesca has a cold and kept us up all night. Brenda has left The Riots, moving down the road to be more ethnic. Her new boyfriend is a Rastafarian version of Wolfgang.

Orders for, *Ireland and Enfields Green* and *Baby Batterers* are coming in, although they are the one or two copy variety. There is however definite movement in the bookshops, but as of yet it is unspectacular. Oberammergau continues to sell gently.

APRIL 22ND 1980

What do publishers do, who do not do their own repping, distribution, publicity and writing? I can't help wondering? For instance, if it is a bit quiet on the sales and distribution front, I turn my attention to the publicity and Mediaville. Then there are the accounts' statements to be sent out. When I have some spare time in the evening or on the tube, I write my diary. It is a full and satisfying life. I'm sure if I were the head of a large publishing corporation I would be bored stiff when I wasn't attending parties and book launches. Looking busy when you have nothing to do is the most soul destroying activity known to man.

My ambition in life is to carry on doing what I do now and get paid for it. Beatrice hasn't mentioned the law for at least a month, which must be a good sign. Better a happy poor publisher than a rich lawyer.

MAY 1ST 1980

Business jogs along quietly but definitely. Each day brings a handful of orders and a healthy supply of payments. By eleven o'clock the office work is up to date and I sit with Beatrice and Francesca in the garden, proof reading Pirandello. It has been decided to delay the publication of Grazia Deledda, and the novels by other members of the Writing Class as Anthony Trollope and Jane Austen have second novels ready. It is these second novels which give me real hope for the future. Both should get reviewed on publication and DEAD LOSS will seem like a real publisher with a proven record of success.

Life is a funny business, when there is no hope at all and things are very flat, something turns up and off you go again. I feel it in my bones, now, that we have made it. Everything is just a matter of time. If the Travel Co. deal works and sales elsewhere keep steady we will have sold thirty thousand Oberammergau books, enough to fund our entire publishing programme for the next two years. At the next board meeting I will bring up the question of a salary for Dante Alighieri and Beatrice Portinari. I can't see how anyone can object as we do all the work. It doesn't look good if a company does not possess any paid employees, is what our accountant used to say, in the days when we had an accountant.

MAY 11TH 1980

I finally pluck up courage and have a financial discussion with Beatrice. As with most of our difficult conversations it took place casually, while we were building a castle in the sand pit for Francesca. Our little treasure's joyful babblings contrasting with the dark look on Beatrice's face.

My beloved said not a word as I announced that my solution to our present financial difficulties was a four month absence, as I went back and forwards to Oberammergau with American tourists. I would earn enough to keep us going for six months, if we were frugal, and then DEAD LOSS would be in a position to pay us a living wage. I painted the rosiest picture imaginable of the future and the success that we could look forward to with DEAD LOSS. How things would get progressively easier as we became known as an imprint and our authors established themselves with second and third novels. We would build up Anthony Trollope and Jane Austen until they were major authors ... Francesca demolished the castle that we had built for her, gurgling in infant ecstacy. Beatrice's smiling eyes were clouded with tears. I lacked the heart to rebuild Francesca's sand castle, telling my little beatitude, that I would build her another sand castle tomorrow.

Ireland and Enfields Green appeared in *The Times*. The review was, as usual, excellent and should sell a few dozen more books. What we need, it seems, are feature articles to draw attention to our amazing success story. But after a week spent ringing Feature Editors I have come to the conclusion we are neither amazing nor by MediaLand's standards, a success.

I am not dejected as Anthony Trollope's second novel is even better than the first. It is as usual incredibly longwinded, and I have made suggestions that would reduce it from its present one hundred thousand words to a trim fifty-five thousand. Trollope said, having butchered the first I can leave the second one alone. Second rate artists should concentrate their mediocrity on their own work and leave the first rate unpolluted by their creative editing. I should, he thinks, become a critic as that is all I'm good for.

There is one overwhelming advantage Giovanni Verga has over Anthony Trollope and his ilk, he is at least dead. Last night I had my Verga nightmare again. This time Verga was in Shakespearean dress and copies of his books in their DEAD LOSS burgundy covers stretched out until the end of time. Giovanni shook his locks at me and laughed hysterically. I was just about to wake up when Toni and his little brats appeared open mouthed to watch the DEAD LOSS books go by. As they joined in the laughter I awoke, yelling foul things at them in my purest Florentine.

MAY 25TH 1980 FRANKFURT

I left at six-thirty a.m. for Heathrow, kissing my beloved little Francesca goodbye as she slept in her cot. Beatrice and I embraced in the way you would expect from a couple who were not going to see each other for four months. Full of, "*ti amo, ti amo tanto*", we were parted by the arrival of the minicab, tearfully exchanging our last farewell.

In the minicab I could not help but reflect on what I was doing. Was DEAD LOSS worth it, I wondered? At that moment I came to the conclusion that it was not and that families must stay together at all costs. The destiny of a small independent publisher is a hard one which only the very strongest should undertake.

I'm on my tenth beer and am full of doubts whether or not I'm made to be a publisher. That single-minded determination needed seems to be missing. Hiccupping I realise my problem and change my order from beer to red wine and tell a smiling barmaid, that I'm a DEAD LOSS and DEAD LOSS is my destiny.

Tomorrow, at any rate I will be on my way to Oberammergau and will be able to see if it is as beautiful as I said it was in the Oberammergau book.

JUNE 7TH 1980

This tour is really exhausting, and is what my colleagues jokingly refer to as a pyjama tour. My only free time is in Oberammergau during the day of the Play. I know I should go and see the Play, but I can't resist temptation and intend to spend the whole day in bed, that is after my early morning walk to sell my own ticket for the going rate outside the theatre. At the moment the going rate is double or if you're very persistent treble.

I inquired of the Travel Co. rep how sales of our Oberammergau book were going. He said they weren't as all ten thousand copies are being held by the customs at Munich Airport until one thousand pounds in custom duty is paid. I try and look on the bright side; there are still almost four months left of the Oberammergau season for Travel Co. to sell its ten thousand copies. I spent my afternoon siesta ringing up Travel Co. in London, but no one will give me a straight answer, even when I got angry and said that I would set the Mafia on them.

Beatrice has promised to ring Travel Co. every day until they pay the custom's duty and get the books to Oberammergau.

JUNE 18TH 1980

Last night was real a disaster, with my hyperacidity keeping me awake all night. When we left Oberammergau at seven-thirty a.m. I was so tired that I was barely able to wish my people good morning. Happily the motion of the coach relaxed me and when we got on the highway I managed to sleep, and probably would have slept for hours if it wasn't for my Verga nightmare.

Giovanni was wearing biblical dress and speaking in German about the foolhardiness of publishing Passion Plays in a world peopled by atheists. He has a horrible laugh, does Giovanni. When I awoke screaming, the driver told me to go back to sleep as it was still a good hour to the coffee stop. I took his advice and immediately went back to sleep, only to find Giovanni there waiting for me. He was dressed as a Lufthansa pilot and was seated on a pile of ten thousand Oberammergau books on the runway of Munich Airport.

It was a very bad day and got even worse when my people got me a cake and we celebrated my birthday at Hohenschwangau. Things, I thought, could not get any worse but I was mistaken. After a party in the hotel bar, Mrs. Boronski's daughter, a quiet, thoughtful and I wrongly believed, shy girl, came to my room and made me the kind of offer it is hard not to take seriously. It took me a full minute before I finally succeeded in speaking, and told Mina that such things were against company rules and that she should put her clothes on and leave.

"You're a real creep Dante Alighieri, a real creep," were Mina's parting words, with a sting in the tale, "even the Reverend is more fun than you."

127

JUNE 20TH 1980

Beatrice says she can manage DEAD LOSS without help, which is just as well, as there is no help available. Yoll roller skates round to The Riots to pick up the big parcels for the Post Office twice a week while everyone else is unavailable. Business is erratic, and on some days there are neither orders nor payments. I worry all the time about Oberammergau and the ten thousand copies sitting at Munich airport, and the ten thousand unsold copies sitting in the spare room.

Travel Co. has said it will pay the custom's duty. So I have some hope that disaster can be avoided. In my four weeks of touring I have managed to sell one hundred and thirty-one books, Wolfgang has sold thirty, so things could be worse.

Beatrice and Francesca are coming to visit me next month, with Mrs. Portinari looking after the office.

JULY 4TH 1980

Oberammergau, the book, has arrived in the village. I felt so happy that I celebrated by watching the Passion Play. It really was very good, especially the music, and well worth the money I would have got if I had sold my ticket. What amazed me most was that the time passed so quickly. I was wrong to think that a seven hour Play in a language I did not understand would be boring. I now understand why so many people come here and why writing a book about it was such a good idea. I feel proud to have contributed to Oberammergau: the book.

It is considered unprofessional by my colleagues to have seen the Play, rather than having sold your ticket for the highest price, so I did not tell anyone that I saw the Play. The Oberammergau book sells well amongst tour escorts, and some of them even sell it to their clients. I have decided to see the Play at least one more time before the end of the Oberammergau season. Beatrice will be here next week, and

I will insist she sees it, while I babysit Francesca down at Mutti Trissl's.

Francesca, Beatrice tells me, is beginning to crawl. Business is up and down still, although repeat orders for Oberammergau are coming in regularly now.

THE FOURTH NOTEBOOK

Unfinished Business

a.m. Giovanni and Pietro have just left. They both agree it is probable I would lose if I tried to enforce the option clause against Anthony Trollope and Jane Austen in the courts.

"It is not," they said, "worth the paper it is written on, and you as a lawyer Dante, should have known that."

I was silent as my incompetence as a lawyer was added to my inability as a publisher. I couldn't think of any excuse, as it was I who drafted the contracts, adapting a standard form contract out of a precedent book. My brothers would have laughed if I had told them I was just trying to be fair. Besides, who would have expected their friends to desert them in their publishing hour of need. In future DEAD LOSS' option clause will be strong enough to keep the Titanic from going under.

Surrounded by Giovanni Verga and Oberammergau wherever I went in The Riots, I reflected bitterly on my betrayal. Jane Austen had gone all feminist on me, while Anthony Trollope had joined the *crème de la crème*, as an interesting little delicacy to bring up the rear of their list.

I have put back all our forthcoming titles until I have decided what to do. Beatrice has had enough and is staying with Francesca at her mother's. She will only come back when our house is free of books. Publishing as far as she is concerned is a Dead Loss, and must survive as best it can without the help of the Alighieri and the Portinari. Even the book by Luigi Pirandello has failed to get her to change her mind. He is, she said, like Giovanni Verga, a Sicilian and not even the Nobel prize can change that.

"They both probably wrote with a pen in one hand and a hammer in the other."

I think it is just a temporary aversion to all things Sicilian, caused by next door's rent-a-brats rioting round her during the Summer.

p.m. Mr. Fashing of, You've got it, We remainder it Ltd., arrived with a big smile and an even bigger lorry. When the ten thousand Oberammergau books were packed and Mr. Fashing gave me a cheque for one thousand pounds, he started giving covetous glances at dear Giovanni and Luigi.

"Ten pence Mr. Alighieri, is not a bad price, you know," he said cheerfully.

I shook my head violently.

"If you should change your mind Mr. Alighieri, you know where to ring."

Before he left I gave Mr. Fashing the Portinari's address and said he could have all the books stored in their garage for ten pence a book.

"A pleasure to do business with you, Mr. Alighieri, you're a real gent."

"If you could do it today, I would be much obliged," I said, as I saw him to the door, anxious to show Beatrice I was doing all I could to get her back.

"Of course Mr. Alighieri," Mr. Fashing said, taking his hat off to Toni, who just happened to be standing outside, and smiling paternally at all the assembled rent-a-brats.

OCTOBER 2ND 1980

a.m. I had a really good time last night. I started reading my way through the piles of manuscripts stacked neatly in the spare room. Normally two pages were sufficient to discontinue reading, and if I were generous a chapter at most, but the tenth manuscript kept me up all night until I had finished it. It was a masterpiece, and I was so excited that I rushed round to the Portinari at six a.m. I hugged and kissed Mrs. Portinari when she opened the door to me. She still kisses with her tongue in my mouth. Screaming, "Beatrice, Beatrice," I clambered up the stairs to my beloved's room.

"We are saved Beatrice, we are saved," I yelled joyfully, as I embraced my startled beatitude, "I have discovered a genius."

I shook Geoffrey Farrington's manuscript of *The Revenants* at my startled beatitude. Francesca awoke to share my joy, screaming loudly in her cot.

"It is, Beatrice, the best Gothic novel I have ever read. It is so commercial, so stupendous that it cannot fail."

Beatrice for some reason got angry, and got even angrier as Francesca's screams grew in intensity. I think she feels that a good vampire novel is insufficient grounds to be woken up for at six o'clock in the morning.

"Dante," she said, when she had calmed down and had time to change from Florentine to English, "I thought we had already published the best ever Gothic novel in Mary Shelley's *Frankenstein*, and it failed. Whatever we publish fails. Enough is enough. Your Mr. Farrington will be published elsewhere. DEAD LOSS is dead and gone. Face up to it, like everyone else has done, and let us live a normal life. You've tried publishing, but it hasn't worked. So now's the time to admit defeat gracefully and become a lawyer."

Tearfully I left the Portinari, aware of the difficult decisions I had to make. If I wanted to see my beloved's smiling eyes again I would have to renounce my destiny and practise the law.

p.m. I was on the thirty-fifth manuscript when the delivery van arrived. With my help the nine thousand, nine hundred and twenty-one Oberammergau books were transferred into the hall and lounge of The Riots. Toni looked like he was on the verge of offering his help if he could only catch my eye. I gave the sweating delivery man a cup of tea while I apologised for not having a fork-lift truck. He was a Geordy and rather jolly, so we graduated onto Chianti from the tea and when Mr. Fashing's lorry from, You've got it, We remainder it Ltd. came, he helped to get the books out onto the lorry. Apologising again to Mr. Fashing's driver for not having a fork-lift truck I invited him in for a glass, and we spent a pleasant afternoon drinking.

OCTOBER 3RD 1980

I cancelled the invoice for ten thousand copies to Travel Co. and reinvoiced them for the seventy-nine they had sold. With the invoice I enclosed the letter prepared for me by Giovanni, in which we threatened to sue Travel Co., for not keeping their side of the bargain, in that, they did not try to sell our books properly, and demanding compensation.

"It was," said Giovanni, "a long shot, but worth trying. If it came to court it would be a very interesting case and if we won, it would create legal history, establishing a duty to try in good faith to sell goods you have bought on sale or return conditions."

The idea of creating legal history did little to compensate for the betrayal of Travel Co. I could still remember that afternoon in Oberammergau when I threatened to kill the Travel Co. rep if he did not try and sell our books. And his reply ringing in my ears:

"You don't sell a book to someone, when they have not got a ticket for the Passion Play they've come half way round the world to see."

Perhaps Travel Co. would settle to avoid the bad publicity but knowing Travel Co. I doubted it.

In order to free my mind from all thoughts of Oberammergau I returned to reading the manuscripts, getting up to the last one by six o'clock. I think I deserve an entry in *The Guinness Book of Records* for having worked my way through seventy-nine manuscripts in two days. I have written to the editor a letter informing him of my unique editorial achievement.

I had little to do that evening so I read through my diary for the first time. It was remarkably interesting and incredibly well written. An idea filled my mind, which despite all my efforts I could not get rid of, try as I might.

OCTOBER 4TH 1980

5 a.m. There was no kiss this time from Mrs. Portinari, who shook her head in disbelief at my early arrival.

"*Amore, sono io*," I sung out joyfully as I entered the bedroom. In my impetuosity I had entered the wrong room and Beatrice's father pulled the bedcovers around him for protection. Apologising I made my way up to the next floor where Beatrice was waiting on the landing.

"For you," she screamed as she flung the contents of Francesca's potty at me. Happily Beatrice's aim is not at its best early in the morning and she missed. I embraced Beatrice, showering her with kisses and would have made love on the landing if Beatrice had not escaped downstairs and barricaded herself in her parents' room.

"Go away *diliquente*," yelled signor Portinari from inside, "before I call the police."

I implored and beseeched an audience with my beloved and her smiling eyes and when I failed to get it, I explained my masterstroke through the key hole.

"He's crazy," Beatrice said to her father, "my husband is a madman. He will never give up until we are in the streets without clothes on our backs."

Mrs. Portinari, with the help of a few good blows from her frying pan, persuaded me to leave. As she saw me out, she said in farewell:

"If I ever see you again at five a.m., I will kill you Dante Alighieri."

I waved good-bye with my tongue out, as Mrs. Portinari closed the door. She confirmed my deepest held conviction that she did not really like me, and that she and Mr. Portinari were doing their best to keep Beatrice and Francesca from me.

9 a.m. I was outside the Post Office when it opened and filled in the Recorded Delivery form in ecstasy. I kissed the three notebooks which I enclosed in the jiffy bag. When I returned to The Riots I rang up the printer and explained the rush job coming up to him.

"I will," I said, "be permanently in your debt if you could typeset the first three notebooks within fourteen days. And then the fourth one as soon as you get it."

Mr. Caxton it seemed was too busy, until I mentioned the cheque for two thousand pounds that I had enclosed with the notebooks. Mr. Caxton then said, as it was for DEAD

LOSS, he would put aside everything else, and it would be done en receipt. Such an obliging man, is Mr. Caxton.

OCTOBER 5TH 1980

The Diary of a Small Publisher was the first title I thought of for my notebooks, but this gave way after a cup of tea to *The Dead Loss Story*. I was quite happy with this title until I had a brain wave. The title had to be *The Dead Loss Success Story*. That was a perfect title if there ever was one. I had a good laugh about that gem of irony. My ability to see the funny side of life has always been one of my strengths.

To confirm the title as immutable, I gave it an ISBN number, and wrote off for a C.I.P. listing. I rang Yoll, who promised to let me have a press release by the weekend. He did not share my enthusiasm for the project and said it was my worst idea yet, which was a compliment as he had never met anyone who had as many bad ideas as I did. Yoll I'm afraid lacks seriousness, which makes him perfect as a press release writer, but useless as a publisher.

OCTOBER 7TH 1980

Beatrice told me she loves me and that Francesca misses romping over Giovanni Verga in the spare room. My eyes filled with joy, and we both enjoyed a very moving British Telecom silence.

"Come home, *amore mio*," I implored down the phone.

"I want to beloved, but first you must promise to get a proper job and forget about publishing."

"*Amore*, you have my word, that I will never publish another book again. But first I must finish off what is in the pipeline. *The Dead Loss Success Story* must be told. I owe it to all of us and all our work, that the world knows the whole truth. We must go out with a bang."

"You promise that this will be the last book, Dante?"

I promised that and a whole lot more besides as my love stretched down the wire to Beatrice Portinari and Francesca Alighieri, before expanding round the room, until it filled the whole house with my heavenly embrace, and danced in unison with the firmament.

The vision of my little beatitude in her adventure play-ground, crawling joyfully over *Mastro Don Gesualdo* on her way to the *Short Sicilian Novels* filled my eyes with tears. In a state of rapture I began calling round Media Land, telling the Feature Editors of this brilliant story — *The Dead Loss Success Story*. Either my enthusiasm or the inherent logic of the idea aroused a great amount of interest. I would need a stunt to go with the idea, I was told, then it was a winner. The mention of a stunt made me smile. I promised a stunt to end all stunts. We have had the birth, and the rebirth of DEAD LOSS, this time Covent Garden would see the death of DEAD LOSS.

OCTOBER 8TH 1980

Beatrice and I spent the whole morning in bed cuddling, with Francesca sharing our embraces. We had decided to spend one day a week in bed from now on. It will be called Cuddlesday, and come between Tuesday and Thursday. At midday the phone refused to stop, so I eventually answered it. It was Wolfgang ringing from Frankfurt. He was very excited and kept insisting that he had sold the rights on all our books at The Book Fair. We had, he kept yelling, made it. I couldn't share Wolfgang's enthusiasm, remembering the twenty thousand unsold copies of Oberammergau we had remaindered.

"Sign them up Wolfgang, and get their money, then ring me back with the good news."

When Beatrice asked who it was, I replied just Wolfgang ringing from Germany to say hello. I had learnt to avoid mentioning DEAD LOSS to Beatrice. If I told her that DEAD LOSS was saved, yet again, I would see my beloved disappearing back to *la casa dei Portinari*. Besides which, the only salvation I could see for DEAD LOSS was the publication of my diary.

OCTOBER 11TH 1980

While I was out seeing a new cover designer, the proofs arrived and Beatrice read them. Instead of sharing my pleasure at the brilliance and readability of my notebooks, she called me the foulest name I have ever heard from such a sweet mouth.

"My life," screamed Beatrice, "is not going to be paraded about in public and turned into a bad situation comedy show. The Portinari would become the laughing stock of Brixton and Florence. Have you no shame, Dante Alighieri, no sense of honour or self esteem?"

"I have all these things Beatrice?" I replied, "and in abundance. The publication of my notebooks will enhance and not diminish the standing of the Alighieri and the Portinari in the world."

"Dante Alighieri you are an incorrigible idiot and a simpleton, and will remain that way until your dying day."

"Beatrice," I replied, "don't speak to me in that way. At least not in front of Francesca."

"The child will learn soon enough what kind of man her father is, although she might forget what he looks like."

"Beatrice, *amore mio* ..."

"If you publish those diaries, you will never see me or Francesca ever again."

I stood speechless as my beloveds departed yet again for *la casa dei Portinari*, Francesca waving good-bye to daddy as they left. I took comfort in philosophy, for one day Mr. and Mrs. Portinari would have left this world for the next, and Beatrice would have nowhere to go to whenever she got in a bad mood. All this coming and going was decidedly bad for our angelic beatitude of a child, and must be stopped.

I read through the proofs, correcting the errors, and then prepared them for posting.

This my fourth and final notebook I will include in the parcel. My beloved will calm down, her temper going as fast as it came, and peace with Beatrice and Francesca will return to the Alighieri home. The publication of my notebooks will bring esteem to the Alighieri and will make Beatrice famous, her name surviving down the generations, to be renowned when our families are no more. Of Beatrice, I will say things which have never been said of any woman. Perhaps it would sound better in Italian:

"*Io spero di dire di lei, quello che mai fu detta d'alcuna.*"

THE EPILOGUE

These notebooks were not published. Signora Portinari says that she was unaware of their existence. What was published on January 15th 1981 was *The Revenants* by Geoffrey Farrington, which became a best seller and a very successful horror film. The success of DL, as the imprint is now called, can be traced back to the phenomenal success of *Ireland and Enfields Green* by Anthony Trollope, which has sold over five million copies in America and nearly a million copies in the rest of the English speaking world. It has been translated into thirty-seven languages so far. The film and television series have made the book and its author household names. The success record with new fiction of DL is truly remarkable and the imprint's efforts to turn the English into avid readers of European Literature is commendable, if as yet unrewarded financially.

The spirit of Dante Alighieri will live on in his, *Comedy*, a book which more than one critic has called, "divine", and in DL, the most spectacular publishing venture this century.

Eric Lane

THE DEATH AND RESURRECTION OF THE NOVEL

Photos by Juri Gabriel